Heartland™

Breaking Free

With a deep sigh Pegasus took a slow step forward and then another, the tips of his hooves on the drive. But then suddenly he seemed to stumble, his feet slipping away beneath him. With a horrifying thud, his huge body crashed to the ground. He landed on his knees and fell almost immediately on to his side.

Amy felt as though the world had stopped. "Pegasus!" she gasped, throwing herself down beside him. He lifted his head.

Relief flooded through her. He was still alive.

"Pegasus! Come on! Up!" Amy urged, pulling his halter. "Come on, boy!"

The great horse looked at her. *No*, his eyes seemed to say, *I can't*. His head sank to the ground again.

Fear stabbed through Amy. She dropped the lead-rope and raced up the drive.

"Lou!" she screamed. "Come quick!"

Other books in the series

Coming Home
After the Storm

Coming soon

Taking Chances

Heartland™

Breaking Free

Lauren Brooke

■SCHOLASTIC

With special thanks to Linda Chapman

With thanks to Monty Roberts, who first wrote about
the "join-up" technique and whose work has made
the world a better place for horses.

Scholastic Children's Books,
Commonwealth House, 1-19 New Oxford Street,
London WC1A 1NU, UK
a division of Scholastic Ltd
London ~ New York ~ Toronto ~ Sydney ~ Auckland
Mexico City ~ New Delhi ~ Hong Kong

Published in the UK by Scholastic Ltd, 2000
Series created by Working Partners Ltd

Copyright © Working Partners Ltd, 2000

Heartland is a trademark of Working Partners Ltd

ISBN 0 439 99804 2

Typeset by TW Typesetting, Midsomer Norton, Somerset
Printed by Cox & Wyman, Reading, Berks.

2 4 6 8 10 9 7 5 3 1

*For Pippa le Quesne — who has made Heartland
a very special place, with thanks and love.*

Chapter One

"Mom's not coming back, Pegasus," Amy said gently to the old grey horse. "She's never coming back." She knew that her words meant nothing to him, but she felt she had to say them – to try and explain.

In the weeks following the tragic accident Pegasus had kept watch for Marion Fleming, standing expectantly at the door of his stall at Heartland, staring down the drive for hours until night eventually fell.

And now, in the last few days, Amy had noticed a change in her mother's favourite horse. Pegasus had become listless and quiet. Instead of looking out over the half-door, he had taken to standing at the back of his stall, his head low, his eyes dull. It was as though he had given up looking for Mom and had lost any sense of hope. Amy couldn't bear seeing him like this. She bent her face to his.

Pegasus snorted quietly and let his great head rest against her chest. Amy closed her eyes. Despite the sadness that hung over him, his huge presence still filled the stall, making her feel safe and at peace, just like it always had. It was the same presence that had once filled stadiums around the world and had made him and her father one of the most famous show-jumping partnerships ever known.

But that had been a long time ago: a time when she had lived in England and when her father had been a part of her life; a time when Heartland hadn't even existed. Amy shook her head slightly. It was another person's life now.

Her thoughts were interrupted by the distant sound of a door opening. Giving Pegasus a kiss on his dark-grey muzzle, Amy went to the half-door of his stall. She could see the slim, blonde figure of her older sister, Lou, coming out of the weather-boarded farmhouse. Grandpa followed behind her, carrying a suitcase.

Amy opened the stall door. "Are you leaving already, Grandpa?" she called.

Jack Bartlett stopped by the car and nodded. "Yes, honey. If I set off now, it will give me a chance to get there in daylight."

Amy hurried down to the car. "Send my love to Glen and Sylvia." She put her arms round his neck and hugged him hard, breathing in his familiar smell of old leather and soap.

"Don't forget to ring us when you get there," Lou said, giving Grandpa a kiss on the cheek.

Jack Bartlett looked from one sister to the other, his

weathered face creasing in concern. "Are you sure you'll be OK? With all that's happened lately I'm not convinced that I should be going."

"We'll be fine," Lou said, her blue eyes meeting Amy's, "won't we?"

"Of course we will," Amy replied. "And you can't *not* go, Grandpa. You know how much Glen and Sylvia always look forward to seeing you."

Jack Bartlett didn't deny it. He made a point of going to stay with his brother, Glen, and sister-in-law, Sylvia, for a few weeks every autumn. When Amy had been younger, she too had gone each year to their farm in Tennessee.

Grandpa was still looking worried. "Are you sure you can cope with the extra workload while I'm away?" he asked. "We're over-stretched at the moment as it is."

"We've talked about this already, Grandpa," Lou said practically. "You know my friend Marnie's coming next week. She'll be able to help, and Ty's offered to put in some extra hours."

"Can we really afford that?" Jack Bartlett said. Amy saw the wrinkles at the sides of his eyes deepen as he thought about paying Ty, Heartland's stable-hand, for the extra work.

"We'll find a way," Lou said, and before he had the chance to speak again she interrupted him firmly. "Look, just go." She hugged him quickly and opened the car door.

"Anyone would think you were trying to get rid of me," Grandpa said, throwing his suitcase into the boot before getting into the car.

"They'd be right," Amy grinned. "We're planning wild parties while you're away, aren't we, Lou?"

Grandpa grinned back. "Sounds like fun. Maybe I'll stay after all." He saw Lou's expression. "OK, OK. I'm outta here!"

He started the engine, and Amy and Lou stepped back and waved frantically as he drove off down the long, winding drive.

"Well," Lou said to Amy, watching the car disappear in a cloud of dust, "I guess it's just you and me now."

From inside the house came the sound of the telephone ringing. Lou's eyes lit up. "Maybe that's a new customer! I'll get it," she said, hurrying off.

Amy looked round the yard. To her left was the front stable block with its six stalls. White paint was peeling off the doors, and the wood around the doorframes had been well chewed by the many different inhabitants over the years. Wisps of hay and straw were caught around the water trough and scattered outside the stall doors. Amy sighed. The yard needed sweeping and the mess by the back barn was even worse.

She looked across the drive to the fields. Horses and ponies of all different colours and sizes grazed peacefully in the September sun. Amy's heart lifted at the sight. She knew that if it weren't for Heartland, most of them would have been put down. Just seeing them all looking so healthy and content made the hard work and long hours worthwhile.

Out of the sixteen horses that were currently at Heartland, twelve had been rescued from abuse and neglect and were having their mental scars healed so that they could be re-homed. Three were liveries, sent to Heartland to have their behavioural problems cured. And then there was Pegasus. He had been Daddy's horse until the show-jumping accident that had led to Amy's father deserting his wife and family. After that, Pegasus had given his heart to Mom. Amy's eyes fell on the empty doorway of the end stall. Poor Pegasus! Without Mom he seemed so lost.

The back door opened and Lou came out.

"Was it a livery customer?" Amy asked, but as she spoke she could tell from her sister's face what the answer was.

"No, just a wrong number," Lou sighed, her eyes scanning the yard. "We're going to have to fill those three stalls soon, you know, Amy. The liveries are our only regular source of income."

Amy nodded. Fees from customers who sent their problem horses to Heartland helped fund the rescue work.

"I just can't understand why the enquiries seemed to have dried up," Lou continued with a frown. "After Nick Halliwell started to recommend us we had quite a few calls. Now there's nothing."

"I could ring him and see if he knows of anyone who might need some help with their horses," Amy suggested. Nick Halliwell was a famous show-jumper. Two months ago, Amy had cured one of his talented young horses of its fear of trailers and since then he had been recommending Heartland to people he knew.

"It's worth a try," Lou agreed.

But when Amy phoned Nick Halliwell's barn, she discovered that he was out of the country competing. "He won't be back for another three weeks," his personal assistant explained.

Amy sighed as she put the phone down. "No luck," she said, turning to Lou who was sitting at the kitchen table.

"It's just so weird," Lou frowned. "We haven't had one enquiry in over a week now."

It was a bit strange, Amy admitted to herself. It *was* rare for there to be no phone-calls for a week. A feeling of unease ran through her, but she pushed it down. "Things will be OK," she said, trying to sound optimistic.

"I hope you're right," Lou replied. "We're going to run into difficulties if business doesn't pick up soon." She sighed and stood up. "Well, I guess we should go and get started on Mom's room."

The breath caught in Amy's throat. *Mom's room.* The words echoed around her head. Marion Fleming's bedroom had been untouched since the night she'd died, but now that Lou's friend Marnie Gordon was coming to stay for a couple of weeks, they needed the space. Lou had decided that the time had come to sort it out.

"It shouldn't take too long," Lou said, as Amy followed her upstairs. "I thought we could divide the stuff into two piles:

things to keep and things to throw away." She opened the door of the bedroom and walked in.

Amy stopped still in the doorway. She had tried to avoid the room since Mom's death, and now the sight of the familiar objects and the faint smell of her mom's perfume caused a sudden wave of emotion to well up inside her. She struggled to control herself. It was three months since the accident, and the unrelenting grief had subsided, but every so often the slightest thing would cause the pain and loss to come flooding back.

"Right," Lou said, walking over to a pile of cardboard boxes that she had brought in earlier. "Let's put the stuff we're keeping over here in this box and anything that's being thrown away over there." She walked round the room and cleared her throat. "I guess we should start with the wardrobe."

Feeling as if she was moving in a dream, Amy stepped into the room. The photographs of horses on the walls, the barn-jacket on the back of the chair, the slightly crooked bed-clothes, the hairbrush with a few strands of hair still caught between the bristles… It was as if Mom was still alive, as if she was going to come walking into the room at any second.

Lou opened the oak wardrobe and for a moment she was stilled by the row of familiar clothes hanging there. She reached out and touched the fabric of a skirt and Amy saw her swallow. But when she spoke again, her voice was practical. "Well, shall we sort through these first?" She hesitated again and then pulled out a couple of blouses. "Anything that's in OK condition can go to the charity shop and I guess we should get rid of the rest."

"We can't throw Mom's clothes out," Amy said quickly. She caught her sister's eye.

Lou frowned. "But we need to make room for Marnie's things."

Amy couldn't bear the thought of getting rid of her mother's clothes just yet. "Can't we just put them somewhere else?" She walked up to the wardrobe and took out a pair of green riding-breeches. Her stomach clenched. She could remember Mom wearing them just a few days before she died.

Lou gave way. "OK," she said, sighing. "I'm sure there's space in the basement."

It didn't take long to pack away the clothes. Amy folded up breeches and shirts and jumpers from the shelves, while Lou took down from the rail the few smart outfits that Mom had owned and packed them quickly and methodically into the boxes. When she reached the last item, she paused.

"Mom's jacket," she said almost in a whisper, looking at the navy riding-jacket with its deep-claret lining.

Amy saw Lou's eyes suddenly fill with emotion and felt her own chest tighten. Mom had given up her own show-jumping career after the accident twelve years ago that had injured Pegasus and Daddy so badly. Amy had only been three and didn't really remember anything about her life then. Her memories started after she and Mom had moved to North-Eastern Virginia to live with Grandpa. But she knew that Lou, eleven years old at the time of the accident, had many more memories of their life in England, memories that the jacket was obviously bringing flooding back.

Blinking quickly, Lou folded the jacket tenderly and placed it on top of the other clothes. Then she started to clear out the bottom of the wardrobe, the shoe-boxes, the bits and pieces of make-up and jars of skin cream. "Look at this mess," she said, her voice tight.

Amy silently took out the jumble of shoes. Among them she found a box. She opened it up. "Photographs!" she said, looking at the two faded blue and gold albums and the envelopes of loose pictures. She opened the pages of the first one. "Lou! It's you!" There was no mistaking the golden-haired toddler who looked out of almost every photograph, cornflower-blue eyes like saucers in her heart-shaped face.

Lou looked over her shoulder. "Yup, it is."

"And Daddy and Mom." There were photographs of their parents looking strangely young: Daddy, tall with dark curly hair; Mom, smiling up at him, small and slender with the same blue eyes and fair hair as Lou.

Amy turned over the pages. There were pictures of their parents' show-jumping yard in England, the horses looking out from around a smart square courtyard with dark-timber stables. There were pictures of Daddy and Mom riding in competitions, pictures of Mom's beautiful bay mare, Delilah, and Daddy on Pegasus. There were even pictures of Lou aged about five tackling a course of jumps on a small pinto pony.

"That was Minnie," Lou said, kneeling down beside Amy with a smile. "Daddy bought her for me when I was three. Then when you were old enough to learn you always wanted to ride her, so Dad bought me Nugget." She opened the second photograph album. "Hey, look! Here's when you were first born."

Amy looked at herself as a baby and leafed through the pages of the album until she found pictures of herself as a two-year-old – a skinny toddler with light brown hair and grey eyes, nearly always pictured either by a horse or on a horse. She looked so different from Lou, more like her father.

Lou pointed to a picture of the whole family sitting on a beach by a huge sandcastle, all smiling. "That was when we went to Spain. You were just three and I was eleven."

Amy turned the pages, eager to see more, but suddenly the photographs stopped. The rest of the book was blank. She looked at her sister.

"Daddy's accident," Lou said quietly.

Amy pulled out the envelopes and tipped the photographs on to the floor. They showed Amy and Mom with Grandpa at Heartland. Amy had grown up by about a year, and Mom looked different too, her face serious, her eyes quiet.

"That's me," Lou said, pulling out a photograph. It showed her standing outside the entrance of her English boarding school, looking very serious, wearing a smart school uniform, school bag in hand.

Amy glanced at her sister. "Why didn't you come with us, Lou?" Mom had tried to explain it to her, but she had never been able to understand why Lou had asked to be allowed to stay in England at boarding school.

"Because I thought that Daddy would come back," Lou said.

"But Mom waited for months," Amy replied, remembering Marion's words. "She said that after Daddy left she waited and waited but nothing happened." She frowned. "He deserted us, Lou."

Lou's eyes flashed. "He was trying to come to terms with never being able to ride competitively again," she said fiercely. "He would have come home to us, but Mom just went and left the country."

"Of course she did!" Amy exclaimed, memories filling her mind of the months when they'd first arrived in Virginia and Mom had been so distraught. "She couldn't stay in England because it reminded her too much of him."

"If she *had* stayed in England then maybe she'd have been there when he did come back and they could have been together again!" Lou said.

But he never did come back! Amy bit back the words. She knew that she had only ever been told her mom's side of the story, but she didn't see that there *was* another side and couldn't understand how Lou could still support their father. After months of anxious waiting, Marion had sold all of the horses, apart from Pegasus who had been badly injured in the accident, and had moved back to her family home in Virginia. There, she had concentrated on healing Pegasus and then started the equine sanctuary at Heartland. Through healing horses that had nowhere else to go, her own emotional well-being had gradually been restored.

"I couldn't have lived here anyway," Lou said. "Mom would have wanted me to help and get involved, and I just couldn't handle being around horses after what happened with Daddy."

Amy thought about the long years of growing up when she had hardly seen her sister, and about the occasions when Lou had visited and there'd been arguments over her refusal to have anything to do with Mom's work. It was different now. Since Mom's death, Lou had rediscovered her love of horses. Amy fingered a photograph of Lou dressed in a long, black university gown, taken at her graduation day in Oxford, England. Standing next to her were Mom and Amy herself.

Lou looked over her shoulder and smiled. "I couldn't believe you and Mom came all that way for my graduation."

"Mom was really proud when you got a place at Oxford University," Amy said. "And when you rang to say how well you'd done in your finals she said that we *had* to be there to see you graduate. Not even Heartland was more important to her than that."

Lou looked surprised. "She actually said that?"

Amy nodded.

"I never knew," Lou said softly.

Amy squeezed her arm. "Mom really missed you, Lou. She was so glad when you got a job in New York."

Lou bit her lip. "But I still didn't come and visit much, did I? Oh Amy, if only things had been different…" Her voice trailed off. Suddenly she seemed to pull herself together. "It's pointless thinking like this," she said briskly. "You can't live a life of regret. You have to move on." She started putting things into boxes again. "Come on, let's finish up."

Amy put the photographs back in the envelope, then she put the envelope and albums carefully back into the box and carried it over to the window. Mom's window, like the one in her own bedroom, looked out over the yard. Pegasus was still at the back of his stall, nowhere to be seen.

"I'm worried about Pegasus," Amy said, turning to help Lou who was now clearing out the drawers of the dressing-table.

"You mentioned that he hasn't been himself lately," Lou said.

Amy nodded. "You know how he used to watch out over the stall door for Mom after she died?"

"Like he was waiting for her to come home?" Lou said.

"Mmm," Amy replied. "Well, he's stopped doing it now. The last few days he's just been standing in the back of his stall looking depressed."

"I'm sure he'll be OK," Lou said, putting the lid on a box.

Amy glanced out of the window, wishing she could feel so certain. "Mom meant everything to him. He must be really confused. Suddenly she's gone and he doesn't understand why. I'm sure that's why he's being so listless."

"Can you give him something to help?" Lou asked.

Amy thought about the herbal and other natural remedies that her mom had taught her to use. She knew several different treatments for grief and loss. "I'll try," she replied. "I'll see what I can do."

Lou smiled at her reassuringly and opened another drawer. "I'm sure he'll perk up in a bit."

They worked in silence for a few minutes. "I think we can throw these out," Lou said, opening the last drawer and pulling out a pile of letters and cards. She flicked through them quickly. "They're just old birthday cards and..." Suddenly she stopped. She pulled out an envelope from the pile.

"What is it?" Amy asked, seeing Lou's eyes widen.

Her sister didn't answer. Amy looked over Lou's shoulder. The letter was addressed to Marion at Heartland. "What is it?" Amy said again, not sure why Lou was looking at the letter so strangely.

"It was sent five years ago," said Lou, looking at the postmark.

"So?" Amy said.

Lou looked up, her face pale. "It's from Daddy," she said.

Chapter Two

"It *can't* be!" Amy exclaimed, staring at the envelope in Lou's hands. "Mom never heard from him after he left."

"Well, it's his handwriting," said Lou. She opened the envelope, her fingers trembling, and took out a letter written on plain white paper. Amy saw her eyes glance over the address. "He sent it from England. *England!*" Lou swallowed. "He was living there all along – I knew it!"

"What does it say?" Amy demanded as Lou unfolded the letter and skimmed the contents.

There was a pause. "I was still *there* then," Lou whispered, her hand dropping to her knees. "Why didn't he contact me?"

"What does it say?" Amy repeated. Impatiently she snatched the letter from Lou.

"*Darling Marion,*" she read out loud. Her voice faded as she read on:

Please write to me, just a note, a card — anything other than this silence. I know I did a truly dreadful thing and I have hated myself every day for seven long years. But please, please find it in your heart to forgive me. We could start again together — just think how much we could do as a team. We were so good together once, weren't we? Surely we could be again. I won't write any more now. Please tell the girls I love them and miss them. All I want is for us to be a family once more.

I have never stopped loving you,
Tim.

Amy let the letter fall to the floor. As she watched Lou pick it up and start to read, thoughts began reeling around her head. Mom had lied to her. Mom had told her that Daddy had never got in touch. And yet here was a letter from him, pleading for forgiveness, asking her if they could get back together.

She looked at Lou. Her sister's face was pale. "Why didn't he try to contact me?" she whispered. "I was the one that waited. I was there!"

Amy shrugged helplessly. She couldn't believe it. Daddy had tried to persuade Mom to give him another chance. And what had Mom's response been? Had she written back? She pushed a hand through her hair, feeling her whole life and all it was based on disappearing like quicksand beneath her.

Everything that she had thought she knew suddenly seemed less certain. What other things had Mom not told her? What should she feel about Daddy, now that she had read this letter?

"Do you mind if I keep it?" Lou's voice broke through Amy's thoughts. She was folding up the letter, her chin set at a determined angle.

Amy shook her head, hardly able to bring herself to speak. "No ... I don't want it." She looked at her sister. The expression in Lou's eyes was unfathomable. "She never told me," she said to Lou.

"She never told either of us," Lou said. She folded the envelope and put it in the pocket of her shirt and then turned to the boxes, her voice suddenly brisk and practical again. "Right, let's get some of this stuff downstairs."

When they had finished clearing out Mom's bedroom, Amy left Lou to vacuum and dust and went outside to see to the horses. It was Ty's day off and there was still plenty to do. Five stalls in the back barn needed cleaning, all the water buckets and hay nets needed refilling and the horses still had to come in from the fields. Amy hurried about, using the chores as an excuse not to think about the letter. Just knowing that five years ago her father had sat down and written to Mom was weird enough, without thinking about the actual contents of the letter.

She set to work grooming and working the three livery

horses — Swallow, Charlie and Whisper. She rode Charlie and Whisper in the schooling ring and then concentrated on Swallow. He was a bay gelding who had come to Heartland to have his fear of traffic cured. He'd been working well in the schooling ring that week and Amy had planned to take him out on the roads for the first time. But what with one thing and another, it looked as if he was going to have to wait. She glanced at her watch. There just wasn't time. She would leave him until the next day. Maybe she and Ty could ride out together when she got in from school.

As Amy led Swallow up to the schooling ring, she thought about how much she missed Ty on the rare occasions when he took his days off. He had started working part-time at Heartland when he was fifteen and a year later had left school to come and train with Marion full-time. He had been amazing in the last few months since the accident. In fact, Amy wasn't sure how they would have coped without him. He worked tirelessly and knew as much about natural remedies and working with problem horses as she did.

At feed-time, Lou came out to help her. "Look at the state of the yard!" she said, as they filled the last of the water buckets.

Amy looked round. The yard looked even more untidy than usual — loose handfuls of hay and straw littered the ground and feed buckets were piled haphazardly outside stall doors.

"Never mind," Amy said. "We can tidy up tomorrow."

"You'll be at school," Lou reminded her.

"I'll do it before I go," Amy replied. As far as she was concerned, a bit of mess didn't matter – what mattered was the horses being exercised, watered and fed. She dusted down her jeans. "I think I'll spend some time with Pegasus," she said.

Lou looked at her. "Have you done your weekend homework?"

"Almost." Amy saw Lou's face. "I've just got a bit of finishing off to do, that's all."

"You're sure?" Lou said suspiciously.

"Positive," Amy lied quickly.

She headed for the tack-room where the medicine cabinet was. Her homework would have to wait. Finding something to help Pegasus was far more important. Selecting three different aromatherapy oils that were meant to help cope with depression, she carried them over to Pegasus' stall, where she noticed that the feed in his manger had hardly been touched.

Putting down the unopened bottles of oil, Amy started to massage the horse's head gently, making small, light circles with her fingers. It was a treatment called T-Touch that her mom had taught her. Her fingers moved over his ears and down his face, sensing where her touch was needed. Gradually she felt him relax.

Giving him a kiss, Amy stopped massaging him and unscrewed the top of the first bottle, offering him the oil to smell. She watched Pegasus' reaction carefully. He put his ears back and turned his head away. She was surprised. It was neroli oil, the remedy that was most effective with horses suffering from sadness and loss. But Marion had always said that horses must be allowed to choose their own remedies and so Amy accepted the grey horse's reaction and offered him the next bottle – yarrow. Again he turned his head away. Frowning slightly, she offered him the third bottle. Pegasus sniffed at it and then lifted his top lip as if he were laughing. He sought the bottle with his mouth.

"No, you don't," Amy said, quickly closing her fingers around the bottle. The oil had to be diluted before it was used. She checked the label – bergamot oil. It was good for balancing and uplifting emotions and was a stimulant for the immune system. It wasn't necessarily an oil for helping to deal with grief. However, if that was what Pegasus had chosen, then that was what she would use.

She took the bottles back to the tack-room and brought a larger bottle of diluted oil back to Pegasus' stall. Putting a few drops on her hand, she started to massage his nostrils. "You've got to start getting better," she told him. "You can't stay depressed like this." She looked at his ageing body. His once dappled coat was now snow-white and his ribs showed slightly. He sighed deeply and her heart ached for him. All her life Pegasus had been there. Whenever she was miserable and upset she would talk to him and he would always listen and seem to understand. Now he was suffering and she had to try and help him, just as Mom had done all those years ago after his accident. "I'll make it better for you, Pegasus," she whispered. "I promise."

The next morning, Amy sat at the kitchen table trying to eat a muffin and do her maths and history homework at the same time. She had meant to finish it the night before, but almost as soon as she had sat down at her desk her eyes had closed and she had fallen asleep on her books.

"Amy! I thought you said you'd done your homework!" Lou exclaimed, coming into the kitchen.

"I've just got a bit to finish off," Amy said defensively.

Lou looked at the half-written page. "A fairly large bit by the looks of it!" she said. "And the bus will be here in ten minutes. Oh Amy, when will you—"

She was interrupted by Ty coming into the kitchen. "Any particular plans for the horses today?" he asked, leaning against the doorframe, his dark hair falling down over his face as he looked at Amy.

"I don't know," Amy said, scribbling another few sentences. "Swallow was really good yesterday, he's ready to go..." she was about to say *out on the roads on his own* but broke off suddenly. "Help! Ty, do you know anything about revolutions in medicine in the late nineteenth century?"

"Sorry," Ty said. "Can't help you there. So Swallow's OK now? What about Charlie and Whisper?"

"Amy! You're going to miss the bus if you don't get a move on!" Lou insisted.

Amy swallowed the last piece of muffin and shoved her books into her rucksack. "Just do what you want with them," she said quickly to Ty, her mind on her work. Maybe she could finish it on the bus. Matt and Soraya could help her.

"OK," Ty said, as she rushed out past him.

Amy got to the end of the drive just in time to stop the bus. Seeing Soraya sitting near the back, she made her way up there. "Hi!" she gasped, collapsing on to the seat beside her best friend. "How was your weekend?"

"Good," Soraya said, shifting along the seat to make more room. "How about yours?"

"Not great," Amy admitted. "And I still haven't finished that history homework."

Soraya shook her head. "One day you're going to surprise me and actually do your work on time." She rummaged in her bag. "Here. Take a look at mine."

"Thanks," Amy said gratefully, getting out her own book.

"So what went wrong with the weekend?" Soraya asked, as Amy found a pen.

"Oh, you know … just things." Amy looked up and saw Soraya's concerned brown eyes. "Pegasus is off his food," she sighed. "We haven't had any livery enquiries for over a week now, Grandpa's gone to Tennessee which means even more work for Ty and me, and then yesterday when Lou and I cleared out Mom's room, we found a letter that Daddy had written to her five years ago."

"But I thought your mom hadn't heard from him since he left!" Soraya exclaimed in surprise.

"So did I," Amy replied. "And he said in the letter that he wanted to get back with her."

"I can hardly believe it," Soraya gasped. "How do you feel?" she asked curiously.

Amy wished she could find the right words to express the confusion she had been feeling since reading the letter. "I'm not sure," she said at last. She paused. "I've always thought that he just abandoned us without another thought, but that's not true and – and—"

"And it makes you think about him differently?" Soraya said.

Amy nodded. "I think so. And Mom too," she added, glancing quickly at her friend.

Soraya squeezed her hand. She didn't say anything – she didn't need to. Amy knew that she understood. Suddenly, not wanting to think about the letter any more, she looked down at the history. "Did you understand the second part of this?" she asked.

Soraya accepted the change of subject. "Yeah. Take a look."

Amy read through Soraya's notes and quickly started scribbling her own answer.

"Have you got anything else to do?" Soraya asked.

"Yeah, maths," Amy replied. "But I was sort of hoping that Matt might help me with that."

"I'm sure he will," Soraya said, giving her a sideways grin. "Matt would do anything for you, Amy."

Amy feigned innocence. "I don't know what you mean."

"Sure you don't," Soraya said sarcastically. She shook her head. "Poor Matt! Every other girl in the school would jump at the chance to date him and he goes and decides that he likes you."

Amy grinned and bent her head over her work.

A few stops later, Matt Trewin got on the bus. He eased his tall frame into the seat in front of them and grinned. "Still doing your homework, Amy?" he said. "How unusual."

"I need help, Matt," Amy pleaded, looking up from the last line of the history work. "I've still got some maths to do."

"OK," Matt sighed. "Where is it?"

Amy handed him her book. He scanned down the page. "This doesn't look too bad," he commented. Matt was a straight-A student who wanted to be a doctor. Amy's report cards were more likely to be covered with Cs and comments like: *Has ability and could achieve more than her current grades suggest.* She didn't mind school – it was just that her school work always came second to Heartland and the horses.

By the time the bus reached Jefferson High, she had finished her homework. "Thanks, Matt," Amy said as they got off the bus and headed for the lockers.

Matt gave a wry smile. "Any time." He left Amy and Soraya to go to his own locker around the corner from theirs.

"Oh, no!" Soraya said in a low voice, her eyes suddenly fixing on a point over Amy's left shoulder. "Look who's coming."

Amy glanced round. Walking towards the lockers were three girls, all beautifully made-up with shiny, perfectly-cut hair and all wearing the very latest in designer labels. The girl in the centre paused. Seeing Amy and Soraya, she raised carefully-plucked eyebrows into an arch and walked over, her pale-blonde hair bouncing on her shoulders. Amy was reminded of a hairspray advert.

"Well, hi there, Amy!" the girl said, stopping in front of her and cocking her head to one side.

"Ashley," Amy acknowledged her stonily.

"So how's business at…" Ashley paused, "*Heartland?*" The way she said it made it sound like some shabby little four-stall affair.

"Fine," Amy said, lifting her chin defiantly. "In fact, we're very busy."

Ashley's lips curved into a smile. "That's not what *I've* heard." Ashley Grant's family owned an upmarket livery yard called Green Briar. Her mom, Val, specialized in producing push-button horses and ponies for hunter jumping, but she also offered a service in curing problem horses. Her methods were very different from those used at Heartland.

Amy frowned. "What do you mean?"

Ashley looked round at her two friends, Sherilyn and Jade, who had moved up to join her. "Should I tell her?" It wasn't a question that required an answer. They smiled at each other.

Amy stepped forward, refusing to be intimidated. "Tell me what?" She felt Soraya move in closer to her and put a hand on her arm. Soraya hated confrontations but Amy's anger was rising swiftly. "What are you talking about, Ashley?" she demanded.

"Oh, just that people are saying that Heartland's days are numbered," Ashley said. Her voice was airy but her green eyes never left Amy's face. "And that now your mom isn't there any more no one is able to cure the horses."

"But that's not true!" Amy burst out indignantly.

"Isn't it?" Ashley laughed mockingly. "Come on, Amy. There's you, that city-slicker sister of yours and Ty. You honestly believe that people are going to bring valuable horses to Heartland now?" She tossed her hair back. "I don't *think* so."

"They are!" Amy cried. She sensed Matt come up beside her. "They'll still come. You don't know what you're talking about, Ashley."

"Oh, I think I do," Ashley said. "The rumours are going round like wildfire. You might as well accept it, Amy. You should sell up. Daddy would buy the land from you." Her lips curved up in a cat-like smile. "After all, our business is doing just great. *Our* barn has never been so full." She winked at Matt. "See you, Matt!" and with that she turned and walked away.

Amy made a move after her.

"Leave it, Amy," Matt said, grabbing her arm. "You know what Ashley's like. She's just doing it to make you mad."

"And succeeding," Soraya said. "Just ignore her."

But Ashley's words had hit a raw nerve. Amy stared down the corridor. What if people *were* staying away from Heartland because they doubted it had a future without Mom? They needed new horses to prove to people that she and Ty were good enough to continue her mom's work. If the liveries stopped coming, then what was going to happen to Heartland?

As soon as Amy got back to Heartland that afternoon, she went to find Lou to tell her what Ashley Grant had said. Lou was sitting at the kitchen table writing an address on an envelope. She jumped guiltily as Amy came in and quickly slipped the envelope under a pile of papers.

"What was that?" Amy asked.

Lou seemed to hesitate for a moment and then shook her head. "Oh, just a bill," she said. She jumped to her feet and started to clear her papers away. "So ... how was school?"

Forgetting about the letter, Amy launched into a tirade about Ashley.

Lou listened intently. "So she says that people have been staying away on purpose?"

Amy nodded. "If it's true, what are we going to do? We can't have people believing that we can't cure horses any more."

"Hmm," Lou said, frowning. "Well, we'll just have to come up with something."

The kitchen door opened and Ty came in. "Hi there!" he said. "Any chance of a hand?"

"Sure." Amy raced upstairs to get changed. It took her less than a minute to pull on her work jeans and a T-shirt. Ty waited for her in the kitchen. "How much else is there to do?" she said, slipping on her boots.

"A fair bit." Amy noticed that Ty's normally calm face looked hassled. "I've hardly groomed any of them yet and three of them still need working. I've realized today just how much your grandpa normally does around here."

"It should be easier when Marnie arrives," Lou said. "She's coming on Saturday and she's keen to help. She used to ride when she was a kid."

Ty nodded. "And being one horse less now will help – although not financially, I guess," he added, glancing at Lou.

"One horse less?" Amy said in surprise, wondering what he meant.

"Swallow's gone," Lou said. "His owner, Mrs Roche, rang this morning and asked if he was ready to come home. She collected him a couple of hours ago." She must have seen the confusion on Amy's face. "You did say so," she continued, uncertainly. "This morning when Ty asked you about him, you said he was ready to go."

"No, I did not!" Amy exclaimed, staring at her. Suddenly she remembered the half-finished conversation they'd had that morning. Her hand flew to her mouth. "I meant that he was ready to start going out on the roads, *not* ready to go home!"

Lou stared. "So he's not safe on the roads yet?"

"Of course he's not!" Amy cried, jumping to her feet in horror. "I haven't ridden him out on them at all. You *can't* have let him go!" She saw the look of shock on Lou's face and swung round to Ty. "Ty!" she exclaimed. "Why did you let Swallow leave? You must have known he wasn't ready."

"But you said he was," Ty replied. "I thought you must have been working him over the weekend."

Amy almost stamped her foot in frustration and worry. "I didn't have time!"

"Listen," Lou broke in quickly. "Let's just call Mrs Roche now and explain." She ran to the phone. "Quick, find me the number."

Amy grabbed the client book and started to leaf frantically through it. What if Mrs Roche had taken Swallow out on the roads? He was better than he had been, but nowhere near cured. *Anything* could have happened.

"Here it is!" she cried, holding the book up.

Just then, they heard the sound of car tyres crunching to a halt on the gravel outside. Amy swung round and looked out of the kitchen window. "Oh no!" she gasped, seeing a well-built, red-faced lady get out of the car. "It's Mrs Roche and she looks really mad!"

Chapter Three

Amy, Lou and Ty hurried to the door. "Mrs Roche," Lou began, "I was just about to phone you. There's been a—" She didn't have a chance to finish. Mrs Roche bore down on her. "I want a word with you, Louise Fleming!" she demanded, her eyes furious.

"Mrs Roche," Lou said quickly, "if you'll just give me a chance to explain…"

But Mrs Roche seemed in no mood to listen to explanations. "I collected my horse from here this afternoon because I was assured that he was cured. I took him out on to the road as soon as I got home only to be almost thrown under a bus. That may be your idea of a cured horse but it's certainly not mine!"

"Mrs Roche, you don't understand—" Lou began, but once again she was interrupted.

"I understand perfectly!" Mrs Roche snapped. Amy could

see the veins standing out on her forehead. "You've been making a living by trading on your mother's reputation without having the experience to deal with the problems you promise to cure."

"That's not fair!" Amy burst out. "It was a mistake! Swallow should never have left. We were about to call you."

"Amy's right," Lou said. "We're very sorry. If you'll just bring Swallow back we'll continue his treatment free of charge." She tried smiling at Mrs Roche but the woman was obviously too worked up for it to have any effect.

"Bring him back?" she exclaimed. "No way! I'm going to take him somewhere where they know about horses." She stalked off towards her car. "And you'd better watch out for yourselves," she shouted over her shoulder as she yanked open the car door. "I'm not going to keep quiet about this, and once I've spread the word you can say goodbye to anyone bringing their horses here any more!"

"But, Mrs Roche…" Lou cried.

The angry woman slammed her car into reverse and, revving the engine, swung round in a shower of gravel and disappeared down the drive.

Lou put her head in her hands. "Brilliant!" she groaned.

"What are we going to do?" Amy cried.

"What is there to do?" Lou said, looking up. "We just have to accept it. I'll write her a letter of apology, of course, but I doubt it'll change her mind. I just can't believe it — this is the last thing we need."

Amy bit back her anger as she saw her sister's shoulders sag. "Don't worry, Lou," she said quickly. "It was just one customer."

"I'm really sorry," Ty said, pushing a hand through his dark hair. "I should have realized."

Amy shot a look at him, frustration at the stupidity of the situation and worry about what it could mean for Heartland flashing hotly in her eyes. *Of course he should have realized*. "I can't believe you let Swallow go!" she exclaimed furiously.

She saw Ty's face stiffen.

"Oh, come on — it's not Ty's fault, Amy," Lou spoke up quickly. "I was the one who spoke to Mrs Roche on the phone. And this morning you did say that Swallow was ready."

But Amy couldn't help herself. "How could you have been so stupid?" she cried to Ty. "You've worked here long enough!"

As soon as the words came out Amy wanted to grab them back. They had made Ty sound like a hired hand. She made a move towards him but he was already turning away from her, his mouth set.

"I'll be in the back barn if you want me," he said, his voice flat.

"Ty…" Amy's heart sank as she watched him stride away. *What had she done?*

Her mind occupied once more with Heartland's financial problems, Lou appeared oblivious to what had just happened. She sighed. "Look, there's no use in us standing around wishing Swallow was still here. We need to think what we can do to make things better. Let's go inside and talk about it."

"I'll just be a minute," Amy said. Leaving her sister to go into the farmhouse, she hurried after Ty.

She caught up with him by the tack-room. "Ty, I'm sorry," she blurted out, putting a hand on his arm. "I shouldn't have shouted at you like that."

Ty's eyes were expressionless. "I'll live."

"But I didn't mean what I said," Amy said quickly. "I really didn't. I'm sorry." She waited, expecting him to smile his familiar grin at her, tell her that all was forgiven. But he didn't – he just shrugged.

"Whatever."

An awkward silence hung between them. Amy suddenly became conscious that she was holding on to his arm. She loosened her grip and let her hand fall to her side.

"I'll be in the barn grooming Jasmine," Ty said flatly. With that he turned and marched up to the back barn.

Amy stared after him in confusion. She had lost her temper with him before, but usually he accepted her apology. He knew what she was like. She said things she didn't mean when she was upset. So why was this time different? Maybe it was because never before had she treated him like a hired hand. Feeling uncomfortable, she returned to the house.

Lou was sitting at the kitchen table making some notes on a piece of scrap paper.

"What are we going to do, Lou?" Amy said, sitting down next to her.

Lou looked up. "If people are staying away because they think we aren't experienced enough, then having Mrs Roche going around telling her story really is the last thing we need," she said. "However, what happened can't be undone now, so I guess we just try and weather the storm. But I think we'll have to make some changes."

"What sort of changes?" Amy asked doubtfully. Lou, with her practical business mind, had tried to suggest alterations to the running of Heartland before, but Amy had fought against them. Still, Amy reminded herself, thinking about the successful fund-raising dance that her sister had organized in the summer, some of Lou's ideas worked.

"Well, first of all I would suggest that we need to make the place look more professional," Lou said. She must have seen the confusion on Amy's face. "Come on, Amy, admit it – the place is a mess. There's hay and straw all over the yard, pitchforks and yard brushes are just thrown into a corner, and the muck heap seems to have a life of its own. What sort of impression does it give to clients who come and look round?"

"It's only because Grandpa's away," Amy said. "Ty and I are just so busy with everything else."

"OK, I agree it's worse at the moment," Lou said, "but even when Grandpa's here the place never looks as smart as it should." She shook her head. "I think we need to give the place a make-over – repaint the stall doors, creosote the fences, reorganize the tack-room, and then make an effort to keep everything tidy."

Amy frowned. She liked the yard as it was. But after the dance she had promised to listen to Lou's ideas. "I guess," she said, rather reluctantly.

"That's settled then!" Lou said. "We'll start this weekend. Marnie can give us a hand. Of course, having a tidy yard isn't much use if we haven't got any clients to come and see it, so we should think about advertising." She turned to Amy. "You remember my idea about having a brochure? Well, I'm going to make a start on it. Maybe that'll bring in a few more liveries." Her face brightened. "If we get enough then we might be able to hire another stable-hand. Just part-time, but it would help."

"It would have to be the right person though," Amy said quickly. "Someone who's into alternative therapies and our way of working." As far as she was concerned, it would be out of the question to employ someone at Heartland who wasn't sympathetic to their mom's ideals.

"Of course," Lou said, sounding surprised, "but I'm sure that wouldn't be a problem." Picking up her pen, she started scribbling a few more notes.

Amy frowned slightly. She had a feeling that finding the right sort of person to work at Heartland wouldn't be quite as easy as Lou seemed to suggest. A lot of people in the horse world were traditionalists who dismissed alternative practitioners as crazy shrink-doctors. She sighed. Right now, however, the problem wasn't about finding someone else to employ, it was about finding some new customers and managing all the work with just her and Ty. She stood up. "I'd better go and help outside," she said.

Amy headed up the yard, wondering whether Ty had forgiven her yet. She found him in the stone-flagged feed-room, making up the evening hay nets.

"Hi!" she said, looking hopefully at his face.

Ty nodded a brief greeting and then bent his head over the hay again.

Amy hesitated uncomfortably by the door. He was obviously still in a mood with her. She wondered what to do. Finally she picked up a hay net and started to fill it. "Lou's been coming up with some ideas to help us get more customers," she said. Ty didn't respond. Amy persevered. "She's going to do a brochure and take it round all the feed merchants and tack stores and places like that." She was aware that she was talking faster than normal, her voice unnaturally high. Ty continued to shake out the slices of hay and stuff them into the net, his head bent. "She also thought that we could smarten the yard up a bit. She thinks it's a mess." She grinned attempting a joke. "How she can possibly think that?"

Ty looked up at her, his mouth set in an angry line. "I've been busy," he said. "There are sixteen horses to see to and only so many hours in the day. But if you're concerned, then I will try and keep the yard tidier in the future."

"Ty, I didn't mean — I wasn't criticizing you," Amy stammered. "Anyway, it's normally *me* who makes all the mess!"

Ty dumped the hay net he had been filling in the pile with the others. "Right. I'll go and start sweeping now," he said.

"Ty!" Amy exclaimed as he brushed past her.

For a brief moment she hesitated. Should she just let him go? But she couldn't. "Wait!" she said, leaping after him.

Ty stopped, his back still turned to her.

"I'm sorry." The words tumbled out of Amy. "I didn't mean what I said earlier. I really didn't. I should have talked to you about Swallow this morning but I was thinking about my homework." She caught his arm. "Please ... I don't want us to argue. You're too important to me." She saw Ty's shoulders stiffen and realized what she had just said. "Too important to Heartland," she gabbled, adjusting her words.

Ty turned and looked at her. Amy hastily let go of his arm and tried to hide her confusion by laughing awkwardly. "I can't seem to keep my hands off you today."

Ty's lips flickered in a faint grin. "I just seem to have this effect on girls."

Amy felt a rush of relief as she realized that he had forgiven her. "Yeah, in your dreams!" she responded. She saw Ty's face relax. "I really am sorry about before," she said more quietly.

"It's OK," Ty said. He shrugged and walked back to the

hay nets with her. "I guess I over-reacted. It's just difficult." He glanced at her. "You know, the responsibility of the place, now that your mom isn't here."

Amy nodded. It was a huge responsibility. She felt it as well.

"Hey, don't look like that," Ty said softly. "We'll make it."

She lifted her eyes to his. "We have to," she whispered, seeing in Ty's eyes the same mixture of uncertainty, hope and fear that she felt in her own heart.

At feed time Amy brought Pegasus in from his field. He walked slowly up the drive beside her, his seventeen-hand frame looking gaunt, his ears flopping listlessly. The bergamot oil appeared to be having little effect. However, Amy knew better than to expect a miracle cure. Natural remedies often took time to work. She fetched the bottle and offered him a few drops on the back of her hand.

Pegasus licked them off, his tongue rasping against Amy's skin. She looked at his ribs, showing more clearly than ever, and frowned.

Amy went to the feed-room where Ty was scooping grain into yellow buckets. "I think I'll give Pegasus a bran mash," she said. "I need to tempt him to eat something."

"Try adding a banana and some honey to it," Ty suggested. "They're good for energy."

Amy nodded. However, even with the addition of some dried mint powder that Pegasus normally adored, he would do no more than pick at the hot mash. She stroked him as he rested his muzzle on the manger. The hollows under his ears were pronounced and his eyes looked sunken. "What am I going to do with you, Pegasus?" she said softly.

He snorted. Putting an arm around his neck she leant her cheek against his rough mane. She couldn't bear seeing him so low. Leaving the stall, she went to find Ty.

"I'm going to ring Scott," she said.

"Good idea," Ty agreed.

Amy went down to the house. Scott Trewin, her friend Matt's brother, was the local equine vet. He was a young vet who believed in using alternative therapies alongside conventional medicine. Through sharing an interest in Marion's work, he had become firm friends with her before she'd died. Amy phoned him at the veterinary centre. He asked a few questions and said he'd come round later to check Pegasus over.

"It's not urgent, Scott," Amy said to him, not wanting to cut into his evening. "We're just a bit worried."

"I'll drop round tonight. It's not a problem," Scott said, his deep voice reassuring. "I haven't got anything else on and I'll be passing."

"Thanks," Amy said gratefully.

At six-thirty, Scott's battered car came bumping up Heartland's drive. "So Pegasus has been off his food?" he asked, taking his black bag out of the car and walking up the yard with Amy. The vet was fair and tall, with a broad-shouldered frame.

"Yes," Amy replied. "And very quiet. I think he's really missing Mom."

In the stall, Scott patted the old grey horse and then listened to Pegasus' heart and breathing before taking his temperature.

"Well, there doesn't seem to be anything obviously wrong," he said at last, "although he's lost some weight. It could be a virus. Any of the other horses shown similar signs?"

Amy shook her head.

"I'll take a blood test," Scott said, taking out a syringe from his bag.

Amy watched the deep-red blood filling up the tube. "Do you think it could be because of Mom?"

Scott considered the question as he removed the needle. "Maybe. Some people would disagree with me, but I believe that horses often do succumb to some form of grief if they lose a close companion, whether equine or human. Pegasus' symptoms are non-specific. They could be a sign of emotional disturbance, but they could also result from a physical illness like a virus, or possibly a more serious disorder."

"A more serious disorder?" Amy echoed in alarm. She hadn't considered the possibility of Pegasus being really ill.

"I'm sure it's nothing to worry about," Scott said. "You'll probably find that he perks up in a day or two."

Amy patted Pegasus. "I hope so."

Just then Lou looked over the stall door. "Hi, Scott."

"Hey there," Scott said, his eyes lighting up. "How you doing?"

"Fine," Lou said. "Have you found anything wrong with Pegasus?"

"Nothing obvious," Scott replied. He repeated what he had told Amy and then packed his things away in his bag. "Well, I guess I'd better be off," he said, straightening up.

Lou opened the stall door for him. "Would you — would you like a drink?" Her voice, usually so confident, caught hesitantly.

Amy looked at her sister and saw a faint blush creeping along Lou's cheekbones.

"Yeah," Scott said with a smile. "That would be great." He walked out of the stall and then, suddenly seeming to remember that Amy was there, he turned to her. "You coming, Amy?"

"I think I'll stay a while with Pegasus," Amy said. She watched as Lou and Scott walked down to the house together, a thought suddenly forming in her brain. Might Lou and Scott like each other? Until recently Lou had been going out with Carl Anderson, a guy she knew from Manhattan. But that was over now. Amy put her arm around Pegasus' neck. "I hope so," she told him. "They'd be just perfect together, don't you think?"

Pegasus lifted his head as though he was nodding. Amy

smiled. She knew it was only because a passing fly had happened to settle on his muzzle, but it seemed like he understood.

"I love you," she whispered, kissing the side of his face.

Pegasus snorted softly in reply.

Chapter Four

The next morning when Amy came into the house to get changed for school, she found Lou putting the phone down — her face worried.

"That was Laura Greene," she told Amy.

"Whisper's owner?" Amy said.

Lou nodded. Whisper was one of the two remaining livery horses. "She wants to take Whisper away. She's coming round with her trailer this afternoon."

"But why?" Amy demanded. "Things are going really well." Whisper had come to Heartland to be backed. After several weeks of carefully building up his confidence and trust, Amy and Ty had decided to get on him for the first time that weekend.

"She's been talking to Mrs Roche," Lou said. "Guess where she's taking him?"

Amy knew from Lou's face what the answer would be. "Not Green Briar?" she said. Lou nodded. "But that's not fair!" Amy exclaimed. "They'll get all the praise and we'll have done all the work."

"I know," Lou sighed, "but there's not much we can do."

Seething with rage at the injustice of it all, Amy marched up the stairs. First of all Swallow going, and now Whisper. And Green Briar would get all the credit.

Her temper wasn't made any better when Ashley came over to her in the cafeteria that day at school. Amy was sitting at a table with Soraya when she sauntered over.

"Hi, Amy," Ashley said, crossing her arms and smirking. "I hear you're going to lose another livery."

Amy glared at her.

"Oh, go away, Ashley," Soraya said.

Ashley ignored her. She was evidently on a mission. "You know," she commented, "some people might say that it's a bit careless to lose two clients in one week. What *are* you doing to them?"

Amy fingers clenched around her knife and fork as she felt her temper starting to rise.

"Mrs Roche is delighted with the progress Swallow has made since he came to us," Ashley said. "I rode him out on the roads yesterday and he didn't put a foot wrong. Of course, as Mom said to Mrs Roche, that's because *we* have the experience to deal with him."

It was the last straw. Unable to bear the thought of Ashley riding Swallow, Amy jumped to her feet. "Experience?" she snapped, not caring that everyone around them was staring curiously at her and Ashley. "He was virtually cured. You didn't have to do anything!"

Ashley smiled maddeningly. "What a shame Mrs Roche doesn't seem to agree with you. Face it, Amy, Heartland's days are numbered — anyone with half a brain can see that." Ashley turned to go, but then suddenly stopped. "Oh, by the way," she said, "did you hear about my latest success? I took home blue ribbons in equitation — first year green hunter and small junior hunter at the Meadowville show. I can't tell you how pleased I was. It's a pity you don't have time to compete any more — you used to be quite good." Smiling smugly, Ashley laughed and walked away.

That night, when Amy got back to Heartland, she found Lou talking on the phone. Her sister was frowning.

"No," she was saying, shaking her head. "No, we're not interested." There was a pause. "Yes, I appreciate that it's a good offer, Ted, but like I say, we're really not interested in selling." There was another pause. "Yes, of course I'll let you know if we change our minds. OK. Goodbye."

"Who was that?" Amy asked curiously as Lou put the phone down.

"Ted Grant," Lou replied. "He wanted to know whether we were interested in selling Heartland's land. Apparently they want to extend Green Briar." She must have seen the shock on Amy's face because she added quickly, "I said no, of course."

"I can't believe that family!" Amy exclaimed, dumping her school bag on the floor. "Why can't they just leave us alone?"

"It was a very generous offer," Lou said.

"But we don't want to sell!" Amy said.

"Hey," Lou said, changing the subject, "we have had *some* good news today. I had an enquiry from a potential customer. A Mrs Garcia. She's got a horse that won't load into a trailer. She's going to call in on Saturday to have a look round."

"Great," Amy said.

Lou nodded, her blue eyes shining with relief. "I gave her a quote. She was very pleased — apparently it was fifty dollars less than Green Briar."

Amy stared. "You gave her a quote?" Her voice rose. "But we don't give quotes!"

"Well, she asked for one," Lou said defensively. "What else could I do? It normally only takes you about a week, doesn't it? I gave her a quote based on that."

Amy couldn't believe what she was hearing. "But we don't know what this horse is like. It might take a month!" she exclaimed. "You'll have to tell her that the quote can't stand. Tell her that we won't know until we've had the horse for at least a few days."

"I can't do that. It's not professional," Lou objected. "We

should have rates and stick to them. Everywhere else does."

"But we're not like everywhere else!" Amy cried, her frustration mounting. "That's the whole point of Heartland. Mom always treated each horse that came here as an individual."

"But Amy—"

"No!" Amy said fiercely. "That's not changing, Lou. Not for anything!"

"OK, OK," Lou said, running a hand through her hair. "I'll guess I'll have to make it clear to Mrs Garcia when she comes on Saturday."

Seeing the worry lines on Lou's face reappearing, Amy felt bad, but this was something she was determined never to give in about. It was one of the things that made Heartland so special – the belief that each horse was different and should be treated according to its needs. She wasn't about to let that change.

On Saturday morning, Mrs Garcia arrived. She was a tall, thin woman who looked immediately put out when Lou explained that the price she had been given was liable to change. "But you told me a price on the telephone," she said, standing in the kitchen.

Lou looked distinctly embarrassed. "I know. I'm sorry."

Amy tried to help her sister. "You see, we don't know how much it will cost until we've had the horse for a few days. All horses take a different amount of time."

"I see," Mrs Garcia said coolly. She turned again to Lou. "So you're telling me that the price might change?"

"Yes, according to how long the process takes," Lou said. "But it might only take three days."

"Well, three days for an initial cure," Amy put in quickly, "but then another couple of days to make sure that the problem behaviour has really gone."

Mrs Garcia ignored her, obviously thinking of her as Lou's little sister and of no consequence. "Three or four days?" she said to Lou, sounding surprised. "At Green Briar they told me it would take at least ten."

Amy had seen her mom cure horses in even less – it was generally easy if you approached the problem with under- standing and respect for the horse. However, she wanted to make things clear to Mrs Garcia. Horses came to Heartland strictly on the understanding that Heartland decided on the type and length of treatment needed. "Sometimes, of course, they can take much longer – up to a month," she said, ignoring Lou's horrified stare, "or even six weeks."

"Six weeks!" Mrs Garcia echoed, her eyes widening.

"Of course, I'm sure that wouldn't be the case with your horse, Mrs Garcia," Lou said hastily.

"But you can't guarantee it," Mrs Garcia said, stepping back, shaking her head. "No, I'm sorry. I think I'll take my horse elsewhere."

"But really Mrs Garcia, like I said it might take only three days," Lou said desperately.

But Mrs Garcia was already walking out of the farmhouse towards her car.

Lou turned on Amy. "Amy!" she said in frustration. "How could you? Now she'll go back to Green Briar and we've still got an empty stable!"

"I only told her the truth," Amy said defensively.

Lou's eyes flashed. "The truth! You did your best to put her off."

"I did not!" Amy protested.

Lou shook her head. "Don't you understand? We're running out of money. If we don't get some paying clients soon then we're going to be in serious trouble. How are we going to feed the horses? How are we going to pay Ty? I can't write cheques if we haven't any money in the bank." She took a deep breath. "Look, if we're going to survive, you may have to forget your principles for a bit."

Amy stared at her. "No!"

"Hi!" a voice said tentatively. They both swung round. Standing behind them was a tall, slim girl in her early twenties, with blonde hair falling to her shoulders in a mass of corkscrew curls, and a worried frown creasing her forehead.

"Marnie!" Lou exclaimed.

Marnie looked from Amy to Lou. "Have I arrived at a bad time?"

"No," Lou exclaimed, hurrying forward. "Don't be silly! It's great to see you!"

"You too," Marnie said, hugging her. "I parked round the front and … er…" she raised her eyebrows quizzically, "heard the sound of voices in here."

Lou grinned. "I guess you couldn't exactly miss us." She turned quickly. "This is my sister, Amy."

Amy stepped forward. "Hello."

"Hi there!" Marnie said with a warm smile. "I've heard so much about you – and this place."

"Come on, we'll show you round," Lou said. She looked at Marnie's smart trouser suit. "Or do you want to get changed first?" she asked. "You might get a bit dirty."

"Who cares?" Marnie grinned. "Clothes can be cleaned. Come on. Show me the way."

Amy followed Lou and Marnie up the yard. She already had the feeling that she was going to like her sister's friend.

They met Ty in the back barn. "Good to meet you, Ty," Marnie said, shaking hands. Suddenly she caught sight of Sugarfoot, the tiny Shetland, in one of the stalls, and gave a gasp of delight. "Isn't he the cutest thing!" The next second she was crouching down saying hello to the little pony. The Shetland nuzzled her face, revelling as he always did in any attention. She looked up at Amy. "You're so lucky to live here. This place is great!"

Amy grinned at her, delighted by her enthusiasm.

"I always wanted to live somewhere like this when I was a kid," Marnie said as they walked round the rest of the yard.

"Where did you live?" Amy asked her curiously.

"New Jersey," Marnie replied. When they reached the front stable block, she looked into Pegasus' stall. "Hey, this fella doesn't look too happy," she said softly.

"He's not," Amy said, joining her at the door. There had been no improvement in Pegasus' condition. He was still off his food.

"What's the matter with him?" Marnie asked curiously.

"We don't know," Lou said.

"He's had a blood test but it didn't show anything," Amy said. Scott had rung her the day after his visit to tell her that the results of the blood test were inconclusive. "I think he's just missing Mom. He really loved her."

"Poor thing," Marnie said. "But he is going to get better?"

Get better? Amy felt her heart skip a beat as she looked at Marnie. Of course Pegasus would get better. She hadn't even considered the possibility that he might not. "Yes ... yes, he is," she said, nodding. She turned and looked at Pegasus. He had to. The thought of losing him was just too much to bear.

Amy and Lou helped Marnie unload her car and then Lou showed her up to their mom's old room. As she unpacked her two large suitcases, Marnie shook her head. "I've brought all these clothes," she said as she hauled one of the suitcases into the house, "but only one pair of jeans and a pair of shorts. I guess I'll be living in those."

"Don't worry," Lou said. "We can always find things for you to borrow."

Leaving Marnie to unpack and change, Amy and Lou went downstairs. A little while later, she joined them in the kitchen. "This is going to be such a great holiday," she said happily. She was dressed far more casually in a pair of cut-offs, a T-shirt and trainers, her wild hair tied back in a pony-tail.

"I don't know about a holiday." Lou grinned. "There's lots of work to be done."

"Lou's got plans," Amy said warningly to Marnie.

Marnie raised her eyebrows. "Sounds ominous."

"Oh, very," Lou teased her. She opened the fridge. "Do you want a cold drink?"

Soon they were all sitting round the table, drinking cans of Coke. "So come on," Marnie said to Lou. "Out with it then. How about this change of lifestyle? It's so totally different from living in the rat-race. How are you *really* coping?"

"Oh, you know," Lou said with a shrug. "I'm coping fine, though I guess I do miss some things."

"I should hope you do!" Marnie said. "All your friends miss you."

Amy felt a bit peculiar. She never really gave a thought to Lou's life in the city now. She seemed so much a part of Heartland that it was hard to remember that only three months ago she hadn't been to visit in over two years and had lived her own separate life – with an apartment, boyfriend and job – that Amy hadn't been a part of at all.

"And having the responsibility of things here is difficult," Lou continued. "I guess it's particularly bad at the moment with Grandpa away."

"But there must be positive aspects about living here," Marnie said.

Amy wondered what Lou would say.

"Oh yes," Lou said. "There are lots of good things. I've rediscovered my love of horses and having a home like this and, well, just being here in the country is great."

Marnie grinned. "And what about the men? Come on, what are *they* like round here?"

Lou blushed. "Oh, you know."

"I want more than that!" Marnie exclaimed. "Tell me all the gossip." She looked closely at Lou. "There must be someone or you wouldn't be turning that colour." She turned to Amy. "Come on, Amy. You'll have to fill me in. Has there been a new man in your sister's life since she dumped Carl?"

"I've been too busy, Marnie!" Lou protested.

"Amy?" Marnie questioned.

Lou jumped to her feet. "We should be helping Ty, not sitting round and gossiping."

"OK then, you escape this time," Marnie said, getting up reluctantly. "But I'll find out," she warned as Lou headed for the door. "Just you wait and see."

In the afternoon, Amy went down to the field to bring Pegasus in. As usual, he was standing by the gate. She called his name, but his ears didn't even flicker. Her heart sank. He seemed to be getting worse instead of better with every day that passed. The remedies just didn't seem to be working. Patting his neck, she snapped the lead-rope on to his halter. "Come on then," she said softly, "let's get you into your stable."

She clicked her tongue but Pegasus didn't move. "Come on, boy."

With a deep sigh Pegasus took a slow step forward and then another, the tips of his hooves on the drive. But then suddenly he seemed to stumble, his feet slipping away beneath him. With a horrifying thud, his huge body crashed to the ground. He landed on his knees and fell almost immediately on to his side.

Amy felt as though the world had stopped. "Pegasus!" she gasped, throwing herself down beside him. He lifted his head.

Relief flooded through her. He was still alive.

"Pegasus! Come on! Up!" Amy urged, pulling his halter. "Come on, boy!"

The great horse looked at her. *No*, his eyes seemed to say, *I can't*. His head sank to the ground again.

Fear stabbed through Amy. She dropped the lead-rope and raced up the drive.

"Lou!" she screamed. "Come quick!"

Chapter Five

Amy crouched by Pegasus' head, stroking him and talking to him softly. Marnie stood anxiously beside her. She and Lou had come running as soon as they heard her call and Lou had gone straight to the phone.

Now she came hurrying back down the drive towards them. "I've rung Scott," she said. "He's coming straight away."

Amy looked frantically at her. "I can't find any bleeding but he might have broken something. I can't tell with him lying down."

Lou took the lead-rope. "Come on, Pegasus! Get up!" But Pegasus didn't move. His eyes were half-closed, his muzzle resting on the ground.

"Lou! What are we going to do?" Amy exclaimed, desperately wishing that Ty was there. But it was his half-day and he had left Heartland after lunch. "He might have broken something."

"Stay calm," Lou said, putting a hand on Amy's shoulder, utterly practical and efficient as always. "You won't help Pegasus by getting worked up."

"But I can't stay calm!" Amy burst out. Her breath was short in her throat and her eyes prickled with tears. "Pegasus! Please get up!" she pleaded.

"Look, I'll get some food," Lou said. "That might encourage him." She hurried off, returning a few minutes later with a bucket of pony cubes. She shook them, but Pegasus' eyes barely flickered in her direction.

"It's like he's frozen there," Marnie said, looking anxiously at Lou.

"It could just be shock after falling," Lou said. "Maybe he hasn't broken anything at all. Amy, what would Mom have used for shock?"

"Rescue Remedy," Amy said.

"Can you go and find some? I'll get a blanket. It's important in cases of shock to keep the patient warm."

Through her panic Amy saw the sense in Lou's words. Jumping to her feet, she raced to the medicine cabinet in the tack-room. Pulling the dark brown bottle of Rescue Remedy from the shelf, she ran back to Pegasus.

Crouching down beside him, she placed a few drops on the back of her hand and offered them to him. His nostrils flared slightly at the scent and then he lifted his head and licked the drops off her hand. "Good boy," Amy murmured, delighted to see him move.

"What are you giving him?" Marnie asked.

"Bach Flower Rescue Remedy," Amy told her. "It's a mixture of different flower essences. Mom always used it for sudden trauma or shock."

Lou returned with a rug and laid it over Pegasus' body. She glanced at her watch. "I wonder how long Scott will be?"

They watched Pegasus anxiously, each second dragging by. After five minutes, Amy was sure his eyes were looking clearer. He lifted his head slightly and his ears flickered. "The Rescue Remedy's working!" Amy cried to Marnie and Lou. She jumped to her feet and pulled on the lead-rope. "Good boy! Come on, Pegasus! Up!"

With a huge groan of effort, Pegasus staggered to his feet. His head hung down, his knees were scraped and bleeding and there was a gash on his right hock, but to Amy's relief he didn't seem to have broken anything. She'd had a horrible feeling that when he stood up one of his legs would be dangling uselessly, but he was standing fairly evenly on all four legs.

Just as she started to check him over, there was the sound of a car tearing up the drive. Amy looked round. "It's Scott!" she said in relief, as the vet's battered car pulled up outside the farmhouse. Throwing the door open, Scott jumped out and raced towards them.

* * *

Half an hour later, Pegasus was back in his stall. It had been a slow process, but once there, the vet checked him over thoroughly, cleaned up his wounds and gave him a shot of antibiotics to combat any infection. Amy watched from the door with Lou and Marnie. As Scott started to pack his equipment away, all the questions that she had been biting back while he treated Pegasus came surging to the surface.

"What's the matter with him? Why did he fall over?" Her voice rose. "What's wrong with him, Scott?"

"He's weak from lack of food," Scott replied. "I think that's why he tripped and why he stayed down. His injuries from the fall aren't serious." He frowned. "What worries me more is his lack of appetite."

"Have you got any idea why he might not be eating?" Lou asked.

Scott looked serious. "It could be any one of a number of things." He looked at Amy. "Remember, he is an old horse."

"What do you mean?" Amy said quickly.

"From his age and symptoms it could well be a serious — very serious — illness."

"No!" Hot tears sprang to Amy's eyes.

"I'm sorry, Amy," Scott said quietly, "but I really don't think his chances are that good."

"He's not going to die, is he, Scott?" Lou said, her face pale.

There was an awful second of silence. "I can't say," Scott

answered. He shook his head gravely. "I could take him to the centre and run some tests but I don't think a journey like that would really be fair to him. We'd be putting him under considerable stress, possibly only to find out that the prognosis was very poor." He looked at Amy. "I know this is hard to hear, but this may be the beginning of the end."

"It can't be!" Amy sobbed. Pushing past Scott, she flung her arms round Pegasus' neck and started to cry as if her heart would break.

She heard Scott turn to Lou. "I think we just have to wait and see what happens over the next few weeks," he said. "If he gets any worse then it may be kindest to consider putting him to sleep."

Amy sobbed loudly. How could she bear living without Pegasus? The straw rustled behind her and then she felt Lou's arm around her shoulders.

"Nothing's decided yet," Lou said. "And maybe he'll still get better."

"He might," Scott said slowly. "In the best case-scenario, his symptoms are simply a product of emotional disturbance. If the depression eases and he gets his spirit back, then he might have several more happy years left with you."

Amy's heart lifted slightly. Maybe Pegasus would make a full recovery. She sniffed and looked up. "What can I do to help him?"

"Try anything you can think of," Scott told her. "You never know, something might work."

Amy nodded. "I'll try everything." She hugged Pegasus' neck. "I'll make you better, boy," she told him fiercely. "I promise I will."

"Come on," Lou said softly, squeezing her shoulder. "Let's leave him to rest."

Back in the kitchen, Lou introduced Marnie and Scott properly.

"Pleased to meet you," Marnie smiled at the vet.

"You too," Scott said politely. Then, seeing Lou trying to carry four cans over from the fridge, he jumped to his feet. "Here," he said. "Let me."

"Thanks," Lou replied gratefully.

As he took two of the cans from her, their hands brushed. Lou's cheeks flushed pink and Amy glanced at Marnie to see if she had noticed, but she had gone to the sink to wash her hands.

"So how's business?" Scott asked, as Lou fetched some crisps. "Any sign of things picking up?"

"None," Lou admitted.

"Well, I have some good news," Scott informed her. "I think I might just have found you a new client, and not just any old client, but Lisa Stillman."

"The one with the Arabians?" Amy said, feeling suddenly interested. There was a Lisa Stillman who owned a large Arabian stud farm about an hour away. Her horses were known throughout the state as superb show horses.

"That's the one," Scott replied. "I started treating her horses a few months back. Anyway, she's got a young mare who's recently become highly aggressive when ridden. I've checked her over and there's nothing physically wrong, so it has to be a behavioural problem. I suggested that she send her here."

"That's brilliant!" Amy said. She turned to Lou in excitement. "Lisa Stillman's stud farm is huge! If she likes us then we could get loads of custom."

"The horse has been to two other stables already," Scott said, "including Green Briar. No one's been able to do a thing with her. Lisa's at her wits' end."

"Hey, Lou," Marnie said, "this could be your big chance. Sounds like if you get in with this woman then you've got it made."

Lou's eyes lit up. "Is she going to phone us?" she asked Scott.

"Well, I said I'd speak to you and arrange a time for you to go over there so she can meet you," Scott replied. "She's quite particular about who she lets her horses go to – most of them are very valuable animals." He scratched his head. "You know, I could give her a call and take you over there now, if you like. I'm going there anyway to see a horse I'm treating."

"That sounds great!" Lou said, but her face fell suddenly. "Oh, what about Pegasus? We shouldn't leave him."

"I'll stay," Amy said immediately.

Scott shook his head. "Lisa will want to talk to you about how you would go about treating Promise, her horse."

"Would you like me to wait with him?" Marnie offered.

"Thanks, Marnie," Lou said, "but it might be better if I stay. Pegasus will be happier with someone he knows."

Amy looked at Scott. She was sure she could see a hint of disappointment in his eyes but he nodded understandingly. "Yes, I guess that would be best," he said. "Amy and I can go."

"Can I tag along too then?" Marnie asked him. "I'd love to see this place."

"Sure," Scott said. "I'll call Lisa right away."

Ten minutes later, Amy, Marnie and Scott got into his car. Amy sat in the back, sharing the seat with Scott's big coat, a trunk of veterinary equipment and a heavy torch. She pushed several map books and a box of medical supplies under the front seat so that she had room for her feet.

"Sorry it's such a mess back there," Scott said over his shoulder.

"I don't mind," Amy replied.

"So, how long have you been a vet?" Marnie asked Scott as they drove off.

"Well, I qualified six years ago," Scott replied, "and then I started specializing in equine work about three years ago."

Marnie smiled up at him. "It must be a fascinating job." She twisted a strand of curly blonde hair round in her fingers. "What do you like best about it?"

As Scott talked, Marnie nodded enthusiastically and smiled and laughed. It suddenly dawned on Amy that Marnie obviously hadn't realized that Lou liked Scott. Amy's eyes widened. She was flirting with him!

"So, how long have you known Lou?" Scott asked Marnie.

"From when she came to work in Manhattan," Marnie replied. "We worked for the same company. I—"

"I guess you know her ex-boyfriend then," Scott broke in.

"Carl?" Marnie said. "Yes. He's working in Chicago now."

"So, are they still in touch?" Scott's words sounded casual but Amy picked up the slight edge to his voice.

"Not as far as I know," Marnie said, looking a bit surprised.

"She hasn't spoken to him since they broke up," Amy put in. Lou and Carl's relationship had ended in a furious row when Lou discovered that Carl had set up a job for her in Chicago behind her back, in an attempt to persuade her to move there with him.

Scott shook his head. "She's been going through a pretty tough time recently, hasn't she?" he said. "What with everything that's happened, and deciding to give up her job and stay at Heartland. She's had to deal with some major life upheavals. But she seems to be coping really well."

Amy saw Marnie shoot him a sideways glance. Realization suddenly dawned on the older girl's face. "Yeah," she said, after a short pause. "Lou's great." Her hands dropped to her lap. "I couldn't ask for a better friend."

* * *

Lisa Stillman's stud was called Fairfield. It was set at the end
of a long, straight drive, bordered on each side by tall trees.
Behind the trees, Amy could just catch tantalizing glimpses
of Arabian horses grazing in lush fields.

They drove past an impressive white house and stopped.
The stalls were set out around a brick courtyard. Purple and
pink flowers cascaded from large hanging baskets. Each
dark-wood stall door had a shining brass nameplate. Stable-
hands were bustling about, each wearing a uniform of green
breeches and green shirt with the Fairfield crest embroidered
in purple on the left.

"Oh, wow!" Amy gasped, getting out of the car and looking at several beautiful Arabian horses looking out over the
stall doors, their ears pricked and dished faces curious. "This
place is amazing!"

Scott grinned. "I thought you'd be impressed." He shut his
car door. "I'll go and find out where Lisa is."

He strode off to speak to one of the stable-hands. The
second he was out of hearing range Marnie turned to Amy.
"You know what? I think he likes Lou!"

Amy nodded.

"You already knew!" Marnie groaned. She put her head in
her hands. "And there I was, flirting for all I was worth. I feel
such an idiot! But he's so cute!" She glanced up at Amy. "Lou
is interested, isn't she?" Marnie said, her voice momentarily
hopeful.

"I'm pretty sure she is," Amy said.

"Oh well, there go my chances!" Marnie said. "I guess that's life. So, how come they haven't got it together yet?" she asked curiously.

"I think it was a hard decision for Lou, breaking up with Carl," Amy replied. "And she and Scott have been getting to know each other slowly."

Marnie grinned. "Well, now I'm here we'll soon get things moving."

Scott came striding back towards them and Marnie stopped talking.

"Lisa's in the office apparently," Scott said. As they walked over to the red-brick building at the far end of the courtyard he said in a low voice, "She can be a bit awkward, so be warned."

They walked into the office where a woman in her mid-forties was sitting behind a desk. She jumped up as soon as she saw them. "Scott!" she said with an attractive, husky rasp to her voice. She had highlighted blonde hair that fell on to her shoulders and a slim figure shown off by tight cream breeches and an open-necked silk shirt. Amy stared. She didn't know what she had been expecting Lisa Stillman to look like, but she certainly *hadn't* expected anyone this glamorous!

"How *are* you, darling?" Lisa said, coming round the desk, her arms outstretched. She kissed Scott on both cheeks.

"Fine." Scott turned quickly. "Let me introduce you. This

is Amy Fleming from Heartland and a family friend, Marnie…" He paused.

"Gordon," Marnie said swiftly.

"Marnie Gordon," Scott repeated. "Amy's sister, Lou, had to stay with one of the horses, but I'm sure Amy will be able to answer all your questions."

Lisa looked at Amy. Her face creased into a frown. "How old are you?"

"Fifteen," Amy replied.

"Don't be put off," Scott said quickly. "Amy knows what she's doing and Heartland has an excellent record."

Lisa turned to him. "Promise is a valuable horse. I'm not letting her go to a fifteen-year-old!"

"Lisa, Amy's got more experience than most people twice her age," Scott began.

"I have dealt with valuable horses before," Amy put in. There was a pause and then Lisa looked at her. "I recently cured one of Nick Halliwell's best young horses of its fear of travelling," Amy said quickly, now that she had her attention. "And I am familiar with all the techniques my mom used at Heartland. She taught me everything she knew."

"And what sort of techniques are those?" Lisa demanded.

"Treating horses with kindness, respect and understanding," Amy said, refusing to let herself be intimidated by the woman's attitude. "Using rewards instead of punishments. Never bullying, never frightening." She put her chin up and met Lisa's eyes squarely. "Listening to the horse."

There was a moment's silence. Lisa's eyes narrowed thoughtfully and then suddenly she nodded. "OK," she said. "I like your attitude. You can treat Promise."

Amy felt an enormous rush of relief. For a moment she had been half expecting to be asked to leave.

"Come and see her," Lisa said.

Amy followed her out of the office and Lisa pointed to a stall a few doors away. "That's her – the palomino."

An exceptionally pretty Arabian was looking over the stall door. A long creamy-white fringe fell over her face, her eyes were bright, her dark grey nostrils delicate and refined. Amy frowned. Everything about the mare's head suggested intelligence, softness and sensitivity. "She doesn't look aggressive," she commented.

"She isn't," Lisa Stillman said, "until you try and ride her. Last week we got her tack on and took her in a show and she tried to savage the judge."

Amy walked forward slowly. Promise turned to look at her. Her ears pricked curiously but Amy noticed that her eyes seemed reserved. Reaching the door, Amy stopped and stroked her gently. "What's her history?" she asked.

"I bought her six months ago from an elderly friend of mine," Lisa said. "She was selling up her stock and I was looking for a palomino. Promise had the perfect bloodlines and the perfect temperament – or so I thought," she added ruefully. "The first few days she was fine. But then one morning when a stable-hand was saddling her up, he told her

67

off for fidgeting and she turned and took a chunk out of his shoulder. When he smacked her she began kicking out. And things have got gradually worse since then. Whenever a saddle or bridle is brought near her, she attacks anyone standing near by and if you try to mount, well, she bucks like crazy."

"But she was OK in her last home?" Amy said.

"Sure," Lisa said. "Half the time she was ridden by my friend's partially blind grandson. Apparently she never put a foot wrong."

Amy looked at the palomino. She was standing, slightly aloof. "And she's been to other stables?" she asked. "What did they do with her?"

Lisa shrugged. "Tried to show her who's boss, but it didn't work. She's got some temper and whips just seem to make her worse. They always send her back in the end, telling me she's a rogue horse." She frowned. "But I don't believe it."

Looking at Promise's intelligent head, Amy didn't believe it either. Her mom had always insisted that rogue horses were virtually a myth. Yes, maybe there was the odd one who really couldn't be helped, but generally fear was at the root of all behavioural problems — and if that fear was dealt with, treated and removed, the problem would go away too.

"So what do you think?" Lisa asked. "Can you help her?"

Amy nodded. Following her mom's reasoning meant that

if she found the cause of Promise's fear then stopping the aggression should be no problem at all. "Sure," she said honestly, "but I don't know how long it will take."

"You can have all the time you need," Lisa said firmly. "I just want her to be right."

"Hi there!" Lou said, coming eagerly out of the house as Scott stopped the car. "How did it go?"

"Really well," said Amy. "How's Pegasus?"

"No marked change," Lou said. "He ate a couple of carrots I offered him but otherwise nothing else to report."

"You should have seen this place, Lou," Marnie enthused. "It was amazing. Lisa Stillman has all these smart stables set out round a courtyard."

"And what about the horse?" Lou demanded.

"She's coming tomorrow," Amy said.

"Really?" gasped Lou, her face lighting up. She turned to Scott. "That's wonderful!" For a moment Amy thought that her sister was going to throw her arms round his neck, but she seemed to control herself just in time. "Thank you so much for arranging it," she said to him.

"You've got Amy to thank," Scott said. "I just put the idea to Lisa; it was your sister who impressed her." He smiled. "But I'm glad that it's worked out," he said warmly. Their eyes met for a moment and Lou turned away, her face slightly pink.

Marnie nudged Amy and grinned.

After checking on Pegasus, Scott left. As soon as his car had disappeared around the first bend, Marnie didn't seem to be able to contain herself any longer. She grabbed Lou's arm. "Lou!" she exclaimed. "That guy's nuts about you!"

Lou looked shocked. "What? Scott?"

"Yes! Who else?" Marnie grinned in delight. "Lou, he's gorgeous!" She shook her head. "I can't believe you didn't tell me about him!"

Lou didn't seem to know what to say. Her face turned crimson. "I – I didn't think there was anything to tell," she stammered.

"Oh, come on, Lou!" Marnie exclaimed, throwing her hands up in the air. "This is *me* you're talking to. It couldn't be more obvious! All he did in the car was talk about you, didn't he, Amy?"

Amy nodded eagerly. "Yes, and he kept asking about Carl – if you were still seeing him."

"And, boy, did he seem pleased when we said that you weren't!" Marnie said. She grinned at Lou. "You're not going to tell me that you don't feel the same. I saw you just now, smiling up into his eyes." She mimicked Lou's voice. "*Thank you, Scott. Oh, you're so wonderful, Scott!*"

Lou burst out laughing. "I didn't do that!"

"Not much!" Marnie teased. "*Oh, Scott, I really don't know what we'd have done without you!*"

Lou buried her face in her hands. "OK! OK!" she cried.

"So maybe I do like him." Her blue eyes shone as she looked at Amy and Marnie. "And you really think he feels the same?" Marnie tapped her nose. "Trust Marnie. I *know* he does."

Chapter Six

As soon as Amy woke up the next morning she hurried down to see Pegasus. He was looking much as he had done the day before. "Good boy," she murmured, checking his cuts and scrapes. They had bled slightly in the night so she fetched some hot water and carefully cleaned away the dried blood. Then she applied some comfrey ointment to help speed the healing process.

"Now let's get you something to eat," she said. "You have to build your strength up."

Seeing her walking up the yard towards the feed-room, the other horses started to nicker hopefully. "In a minute," she told them. On this occasion, Pegasus had to have her undivided attention.

She chopped up three apples, added a small amount of bran and barley, and mixed everything up in a bucket with some beet juice and a spoonful of molasses. Then she hurried back to Pegasus' stall. He stared listlessly at the food and made no attempt to eat, so she took a handful and offered it to him. His lips grazed over her palm, taking up a piece of apple and some bran. "Good boy," she praised. She fed him a bit more and then a bit more. After twenty minutes he had just about finished the bucket. Feeling more hopeful, Amy patted him and then went to feed the other horses.

Just as she started filling the water buckets, Ty arrived. "Morning!" he called, getting out of his car.

"What are you doing here?" Amy asked in surprise. It was Sunday — his day off.

"I thought you might need a hand with the painting," he said, joining her at the tap. "I told Lou I'd come and help."

With everything that had happened the day before, it had slipped Amy's mind that today they were supposed to start painting and smartening the place up.

"You'd forgotten, hadn't you?" Ty said, looking at her face.

"Kind of," she admitted, "but so much has been happening." She realized that Ty didn't know about the events of the day before. As the water buckets filled, she told him about Pegasus' fall and then about Lisa Stillman and Promise. It was a relief to be able to talk. That was the good thing about Ty — he always understood.

When she had finished, Ty helped her distribute the water buckets amongst the stalls and then they went down to the house to talk to Lou about her plans. She and Marnie were in the kitchen washing up the breakfast dishes.

"So, what do you want us to do?" Amy asked, opening the biscuit jar and offering it to Ty before taking one herself.

"I thought if you two got on with the stalls and turning the horses out, then I could go and collect the paint and some brushes," Lou said.

"I'll help with the horses too," Marnie offered.

Lou nodded. "When I get back we can paint the stable doors and then start clearing out the tack- and rug-rooms."

"If you get some wood I'll make some new storage trunks for the rugs and grooming kits and small bits of tack," Ty said. "That will help tidy things up in there."

"Brilliant," Lou said. "Then I might get some new feed-buckets and hay nets. They're not too expensive and they'll give a better impression to new clients."

"How about some hanging baskets?" Marnie said. "Just two maybe, at each end of the front barn. You can put together really pretty ones, even with cheap plants."

Amy started to feel quite enthusiastic. She had thought that she didn't want any changes, but all these ideas would make Heartland look much better. "I'll ring Soraya and Matt," she said. "I bet they'll come and help. We can give the yard a proper sweep and tidy up all the pitchforks and brooms. It's going to look great!"

By lunchtime Heartland was a hive of activity. Amy and

Soraya were busy painting the stall doors white while Lou and Matt freshened up the unpainted wood in the two barns with dark brown creosote. The tack-room had been turned out and swept and Ty was busy making large trunks to hold all the bits and pieces that tended to get left in a heap on the floor – brushing boots, stable bandages, tailguards. Marnie had filled two hanging baskets with red and yellow blooms and was sorting out the grooming kits, washing the brushes and removing old hair caked in the curry-combs.

Amy put a last brushload of paint on to the stall door she was working on and then stood back to admire her handiwork. "Another one finished!"

"Everything is looking so much better," Soraya said, putting her brush down. She looked at Amy. "Which is more than can be said for you!"

Amy grinned. She had started off applying the paint carefully but had soon got bored and started slapping it on. Her jeans and T-shirt were covered with white splashes and she was sure there was probably some in her hair.

"It doesn't come off, you know," Soraya pointed out.

"Who cares?" Amy shrugged. "These jeans are old anyway."

Soraya shook her head and, picking up her brush, started to finish the last bit of the door she was painting. "So what was Fairfield like?" She was as mad about horses as Amy and knew all about Lisa Stillman and her prize-winning Arabians.

"Very stylish," Amy said, and she told Soraya about the

stable-hands all dressed in green with the stud logo, the beautiful horses and the spotless courtyard.

"Is Lisa Stillman going to bring the horse here herself?" Soraya asked.

"She didn't say," Amy said. She wondered what Lisa would think of Heartland if she did come. Promise was due to arrive about four o'clock. She hoped they would have finished working on the yard by then.

"And the horse is coming because she's aggressive?" Soraya asked.

"Just when she's being ridden," Amy explained. "I think it's because something's frightened her in the past. She didn't look like a naturally aggressive horse." She saw that Soraya's door was just about done. "Shall we go and start on the rug-room? There's loads to sort out in there."

By four o'clock, the paint was almost dry, the rug-room was sorted and the tack had been put neatly away. New trunks lined the back wall of the tack-room, the bridles hung neatly on their correct pegs, and the halters were untangled with their lead-ropes tightly coiled. There were still a few things to do – the muck heap needed tidying and the feed-room still hadn't been swept or de-cobwebbed – but overall there was a vast improvement.

Amy stood drinking a Coke with the others by the farmhouse and admiring the bright white doors set against the dark wood, the hanging baskets filled with fresh flowers, and a yard that for once was almost free of hay and straw.

"Now we've just got to keep it like this," Lou said with a sigh of relief.

"Some chance with Amy around!" Matt joked.

Amy hit him. "Hey!"

There was the sound of a vehicle coming up the drive. They all turned to see a smart trailer with green and purple stripes heading towards them. "This must be Promise!" Amy said.

The trailer stopped just in front of them. The driver's door of the pick-up was flung open and out jumped a tall, blond-haired boy. "Hey there!" he said, looking a bit surprised to see such a crowd.

"Hi!" Amy said. She felt slightly disappointed to see that the boy was on his own. After all their work, she would have liked Lisa Stillman to have seen Heartland. She stepped forward. "I'm Amy."

The boy smiled. "Pleased to meet you, Amy," he said, holding out his hand. "I'm Ben Stillman. I'm delivering Promise for my aunt."

So that was why he looked somehow familiar! Amy shook his hand and introduced everyone else. "We've been painting," she explained, suddenly realizing what a mess she must look.

"I'd sort of gathered," Ben said with a grin. He moved towards the trailer. "Should I unload Promise here?"

Amy nodded. "Yeah, that would be fine."

"Do you want a hand?" Ty offered.

"Thanks," Ben replied.

"He's cute!" Soraya hissed to Amy, as Ben and Ty walked round the trailer to unbolt the ramp.

"I guess," Amy said, looking at Ben and feeling slightly surprised.

"Very cute!" Soraya said with a giggle, as he disappeared into the trailer.

There was a clatter of hooves and Ben came out of the trailer, leading Promise. Amy caught her breath, all thoughts of Ben far from her mind. The mare pranced down the ramp like a ballet dancer. Her neck was arched, her golden coat gleamed and her creamy-white tail floated behind her like a waterfall. Reaching the ground she stopped and snorted, wide nostrils flaring, soft dark eyes staring round in surprise.

"She's gorgeous!" Amy breathed.

She glanced at Ty to see his reaction. He was nodding appreciatively.

The mare whinnied loudly and then tossed her head and swung her quarters round. "Easy now," Ben said, patting her neck. He turned to Amy. "Where should I put her?"

"Over here," Amy said, leading the way to one of the empty stalls in the front block. Promise pranced in after him.

"High-spirited," Ty commented.

"Most Arabians are," Ben said, unclipping her lead-rope.

"She's OK — as long as you don't bring a saddle or bridle anywhere near her."

Promise looked over the stall door. Amy stroked her nose, admiring her dished face.

"I hope you can do something with her," Ben said. "You may be her last chance."

After seeing Promise settle in, Ben left. Ty was going home and offered Soraya and Matt a lift.

"Thanks for all your help!" Amy called as they all got into Ty's car. "See you tomorrow."

"Well, I could do with a long bath and a change of clothes," Marnie said, looking down at her filthy jeans.

"Me too," Lou said. She looked at Amy. "But do you want a hand feeding the horses?"

"No, I'll be fine," Amy said. Ty had found time in the afternoon to make up the hay nets and tidy the beds.

"I'll get some supper organized then," Lou said. "Coming, Marnie?"

They walked off into the house and Amy made her way up the yard, enjoying the peace and quiet. It had been a hectic day. She stopped to check on Promise. The mare was standing at the back of her stall, pulling hay from the net. Hearing Amy's footsteps, she looked round.

"Hey there, girl!" Amy said, letting herself into the stall. Promise looked at her for a moment and then continued to eat. Amy stood back, studying the mare. Her mom had always believed that a horse's personality could be read in its face. Amy looked at the mare's eyes. They were large, soft and slightly triangular – thoughtful eyes, highly intelligent eyes. In fact, she thought, everything about Promise suggested intelligence. Her gaze wandered over Promise's delicate, fluted nostrils, shapely ears and dished face with a slight moose nose. All of those features suggested that here was a horse who was alert, sensitive and proud. A horse who would be fabulous to ride. One thing was for sure, she certainly did *not* look naturally aggressive.

It had to be fear that was causing her to act so out of character, Amy thought. When a horse was scared there were only three things it could do: flee, freeze or fight. Looking at the pride and self-awareness mirrored in every line of Promise's beautiful head, it wasn't hard to believe that she had chosen to fight.

"Well, there's no need to fight me," she said, patting the mare's shoulder. "I won't hurt you or make you scared."

She left the stall, sensing the first flicker of excitement that she always felt when faced with the challenge of a new horse. She would make Promise ridable and show everyone that Heartland could run just as it always had, curing the horses that the rest of the world had given up on.

Suddenly feeling optimistic, she went to the feed-room and began to mix up the feeds. Maybe things were finally getting better, she thought as she added handfuls of soaked beet pulp to the grain in the buckets. The yard was looking wonderful, if she cured Promise then Lisa Stillman was bound to bring Heartland more custom, and she and Lou seemed to be getting on just fine. Yes, life was looking up at last.

Amy started to pile the buckets up and then remembered Pegasus. Her new-found optimism faded slightly as she thought about the old grey horse.

She fed the other horses and then took Pegasus' bucket round to his stall. He was standing quietly, his head low, his eyes depressed.

"Hey, boy!" she said, looking over the door.

Hearing her voice, Pegasus lifted his head slightly. "I've brought you some supper," she said, letting herself into the stall.

Pegasus looked at the offered bucket, nudged his lips disinterestedly over the metal handle and then dropped his head to the straw again.

"Come on, eat!" Amy urged, holding a handful of the feed by his nose.

With a sigh, Pegasus' lips moved over her hand taking up some of the grain. Again, Amy fed him handful by slow handful. Pegasus ate listlessly, appearing to eat more to please her than out of any real sense of hunger. Amy consoled herself with the thought that at least he *was* eating something.

She kissed his forehead, willing him to recover, desperately searching in her mind for something more that she could do.

When he had finished the last handful of feed she began to massage his head and neck with T-Touch circles. Pegasus rested his muzzle on his manger by the window and half closed his eyes.

"You like this, don't you?" Amy murmured. She swallowed as she remembered how Mom used to stand in this exact place, massaging Pegasus in the same way. Through the stall window she could see the evening shadows lengthening, and as she worked she thought of all the times when she had come out and watched Mom work her magic.

The minutes passed, her fingers moved over Pegasus' neck, and she felt herself relaxing. As the light in the stall began to fade it was as if the rest of the world had slipped away, leaving her and Pegasus alone, like it had once been just Mom and Pegasus. In the sweet-smelling stall the past and the present seemed to merge into one.

Suddenly every muscle in Pegasus' body tensed. His head shot up and he stared out of the window.

"What's the matter?" Amy said, following his gaze into the dusk.

She gasped, her heart standing still.

There — walking up the yard, hands in her barn-coat pockets — was her mom.

Chapter Seven

"Mom!" Amy whispered, her insides turning to ice as the figure walked towards her through the dusk. Without thinking, she flew to the stall door. *Could it be?*

Wrenching the bolt back with her trembling fingers she stumbled out.

"Amy?"

Amy stopped in her tracks, feeling as if someone had just tipped a bucket of cold water over her. It was Marnie hurrying towards her. Her hair was tied back and she was wearing Marion's old barn-jacket.

"Are you OK?" the older girl asked, looking at her shocked face in surprise. She followed Amy's gaze and looked down at the jacket. "Is it the jacket? Lou said I could borrow it."

Amy's mouth opened but she couldn't speak.

Marnie moved swiftly to her side. "I'll take it off if it upsets you. I'm really, really sorry."

"I — I thought you were Mom." The words came out of Amy before she could stop them. She stared at Marnie, tears filling her eyes. For a moment she had actually allowed herself to hope … to believe… She started to shake uncontrollably.

Marnie quickly put her arms round her. "Hey, it's OK," she soothed.

"In the dusk you looked just like her," Amy sobbed, disappointment and loss overwhelming her. "I — I really thought…"

Just then there was a low whicker. Amy swung round. Pegasus had come to the stall door. His ears were pricked and he was looking at Marnie. He tossed his head up and down.

"Pegasus?" Amy said, forgetting her own distress in her astonishment at seeing him look so animated. He pushed against the door.

"He can't think I'm your mom, surely?" Marnie said.

Amy's eyes widened with sudden realization. "It's the jacket!" she exclaimed. "It must smell of Mom."

Pegasus whickered again.

Marnie walked slowly up to his stall. Lowering his head, Pegasus explored the jacket with his muzzle, breathing in and out in sharp, eager bursts. Marnie reached out and stroked his face. "I think you're right," she said to Amy. "He must remember."

"He looks almost happy again," Amy said wonderingly. It was true. As Pegasus nuzzled the jacket a kind of peace seemed to creep into his eyes. The tears dried on Amy's face. Suddenly she didn't care that it had been Marnie wearing her mom's jacket. Nothing mattered except the fact that Pegasus was looking like his old self again.

Lying in bed that night, Amy found it difficult to get to sleep. She kept seeing the image of her mother walking across the yard and Pegasus' reaction to it. Her hopes rose. When she and Marnie had left his stall he had been looking much perkier. Maybe this was the breakthrough that she had been so desperately hoping for. Maybe now he would start to eat properly and get better.

She hurried out to feed the horses the next morning. However, although Pegasus' eyes looked brighter, she found him as reluctant to eat as ever.

Her heart sank. "Come on, boy," she encouraged him, holding out a handful of feed, but instead of eating he simply nudged at the grain with his lips, spilling it into the straw.

In the end Amy had to give up. Time was moving on and she had to get ready for school. But still she kept hoping. "Can you keep an eye on Pegasus today?" she asked Ty, before she went to catch the bus. "I think he might start eating again."

"Sure," Ty nodded. "Have a good day at school."

"Yeah, as if that's likely," Amy replied, pulling a face. She threw her rucksack on to her shoulder. "See you later."

As Amy walked along the corridor to get to her first class, she met Ashley coming in the opposite direction. Amy tried to ignore her but Ashley stepped into her path, glossy platinum hair falling to her shoulders.

"What's this people have been saying about you having one of Lisa Stillman's horses?" she demanded, crossing her arms. "Is it true?"

"Yeah," Amy replied, lifting her chin. "What's it to you?"

Ashley's green eyes looked incredulous. "Lisa Stillman must have gone crazy. What's she doing sending one of her horses to Heartland? They're valuable!"

"She's heard that we actually cure horses," Amy snapped, infuriated by Ashley's attitude, "which is more than *you* apparently managed to do when Promise came to you."

Ashley's arched eyebrows raised. "So it's that palomino?" She must have seen from Amy's expression that it was, because her perfectly made-up face suddenly creased into a smile. "OK," she said, nodding. "Now I get it."

"What do you mean?" Amy demanded.

"Well," Ashley replied, "it's not as if Lisa Stillman's letting you have one of her *valuable* horses. Everyone knows that palomino is a hopeless case. She's savage. Mom tried everything with her but she never gave in, she just fought like crazy. She needs a bullet through her head."

"She does not!" Amy exclaimed furiously.

"Like you're going to be able to cure her."

"I am!"

Ashley laughed mockingly. "In your dreams, Amy!"

Feeling the anger inside her reaching boiling point, Amy pushed past Ashley.

"You'll never do it," Ashley called after her, her voice amused. "You haven't got the experience to cure any horse, let alone one like that."

Amy marched along the corridor, determined not to listen to Ashley any longer. Her words weren't true. She *was* going to cure Promise. She had never felt so determined about anything in her life before.

As soon as Amy got home from school that afternoon she went to find Ty. He was cleaning bridles in the tack-room. "How's Pegasus been?" she asked.

"No change really," Ty replied. He looked at her curiously. "What made you think he'd be different?"

Amy told him about the incident with the coat the evening before. "I thought it might make him start eating again," she sighed, "but obviously not."

They were silent for a minute or two. "Are you going to work Promise this afternoon?" Ty asked.

Amy nodded. "I thought I'd join-up with her first and then see how she reacts to the saddle and bridle," she said. Join-up was a technique used to build up a horse's trust; Marion had always used it as the first step in the rehabilitation of a horse and she had taught it to Amy. "What do you think? I'm sure she's unmanageable just because she's scared. If I join-up with her, hopefully she'll trust me enough to let me get the tack on."

"Sounds good to me. I'll come along and give you a hand, if you want," Ty offered.

"I'd like that," Amy said with a grateful smile.

Twenty minutes later Amy led Promise into the circular schooling ring at the top of the yard. The mare walked eagerly beside her, her steps short and fast, her eyes swivelling from side to side as she took in the unfamiliar surroundings.

Ty followed some distance behind with the saddle and bridle. Shutting the gate, Amy unclipped the long-line from Promise's halter. Feeling herself free, the Arabian shied away then cantered a few paces and stopped dead a few metres from Amy. She sniffed at the sand.

With the long-line coiled in her hand, Amy clicked her tongue and swept it towards the mare's hindquarters. Snorting wildly, Promise leapt into a high-headed canter. Amy moved quickly to the centre of the ring and, by positioning her shoulders square to the mare's and pitching the long-line at the mare's rump, she urged her on at a canter. She knew that a horse's basic instinct was to see humans as predators and to run away if there was space to run. What Promise would learn through join-up was that Amy was a human who could understand her body language and be trusted.

After Promise had cantered round for several minutes, Amy changed her position so that she was slightly in front of the horse. Immediately Promise jerked to a halt and then swirled round and set off in the opposite direction. Amy's eyes were fixed on the mare's. Soon she saw the palomino's head starting to lower slightly and her muscles relax as the canter became smoother, the strides more rhythmical.

Urging her on still, Amy watched for the first signals of communication that the mare would send through her body language. After five or six circles the first one came as Promise's inside ear stopped moving, pointing slightly towards Amy. It was a signal that she would like to slow down and not work so hard. But for the moment Amy kept her going, watching for the next signal. With most horses it took a few circuits but almost immediately Promise's head began to tilt, bringing it closer to the centre of the circle and closer to Amy. After a few more steps she lowered her head and neck, opening her mouth and looking as if she was chewing. It was her way of saying that she would like to stop.

Quickly coiling in the line, Amy dropped her eyes from Promise's and turned her shoulders round. She stood and waited, trying not to tense up. She heard the soft thud of hooves on the sand behind her and the sound of the mare's breathing. She stepped away and then paused. Suddenly she felt Promise's nose on her shoulder and warm breath on her neck. It was join-up!

Turning slowly and keeping her eyes lowered, because only predators stare, Amy rubbed the palomino between the eyes and then, turning away, she walked across the ring. She listened hard. Would Promise follow her? If she didn't, then she would have to put her back to work and try again. But there was no need. After the slightest hesitation the mare followed her. Amy walked in a circle and, with the mare following her every footstep, changed direction. At last she stopped and rubbed Promise's head again.

"Good girl," she praised. The mare pushed her nose gently against her and then lifted her muzzle to Amy's face, snorting inquisitively. Amy smiled and rubbed her golden neck before turning to Ty, who was standing at the gate. "She was very quick to respond."

"She's highly sensitive," Ty said. "She seemed to know that you were communicating with her straight away."

"That's what I thought," Amy said.

They exchanged smiles. Amy felt a warm glow of happiness spread through her.

Turning back to Promise, she started on the next stage of her plan. She ran her hands over the mare's neck, withers, back, hips and flanks – all the vulnerable areas that a horse would be uneasy about letting a predator near. Promise stood rock-solid.

Feeling confident, Amy snapped the long-line on to Promise's halter and called to Ty to bring the tack into the ring. Now that Promise trusted her, she was sure that the mare would accept the saddle and bridle.

But as she stepped forward to take the saddle from Ty, Promise suddenly exploded. Pulling back, she reared up on her hind legs, her front hooves lashing angrily through the air. Amy leapt back just in time. Dropping the saddle on the floor she moved quickly to the mare's shoulder, closing in on her head the instant her hooves touched the ground. "Easy now," she said. "Easy." For a moment Promise's eyes seemed to flash and she fought Amy's hold on her halter, but then she settled.

Glancing round Amy saw to her relief that Ty had acted quickly, whisking the saddle well out of the way. Leaving it over the gate he now came back to her. "That was unexpected," he said breathlessly.

Amy nodded, feeling confused. She was sure that the join-up had gone well and that Promise had seemed to have no fear of her, so why had the appearance of the saddle provoked such a violent reaction?

"I'll send her round again," she said, unclipping the long-line.

Ty moved to the side and Amy sent Promise around the ring once more. The join-up was even quicker this time. Within two circuits Promise was licking her lips and lowering her head, asking permission to stop. As soon as

Amy coiled the long-line and turned her shoulders, Promise joined her and followed her trustingly around the ring.

Ty brought the saddle over. Almost immediately Promise was on her back legs, rearing and striking out. Ty backed off hastily.

"I can't understand it," Amy said when Promise was standing still beside her again.

"Maybe it's a physical problem," Ty speculated, joining her without the saddle this time. Promise bent her head towards him. "Perhaps the saddle hurts her."

Amy shook her head. "Scott said that he's checked her over really thoroughly and there's nothing wrong. It has to be fear." She frowned. "So what do we do now?"

"We could leave an old saddle in her stall," Ty suggested. "That way she'll see it all the time and get used to it."

"Good idea," Amy said, nodding quickly. "If we leave it there overnight then we can try again tomorrow."

"And we'll give her a little powdered valerian in her feed," Ty said. "That should help relax and calm her."

Amy started to lead Promise towards the gate. "It's funny," she said, looking at the mare's intelligent head, "she doesn't look the fearful type and she seems confident about everything else."

"Fear's like that though," Ty commented. "Horses can have irrational phobias, just like humans."

Amy nodded. She guessed he was right, and yet something about the way the mare had reared up bothered her. She went over the moment in her mind. As the mare had struck out, Amy had caught a glimpse of her eyes and *they hadn't looked scared*.

Amy pushed the thought away. Of course it was fear — fear was at the root of nearly all behaviour problems. That's what Mom had always said. She had also said never rush a horse. Amy knew they just had to be patient. They would work Promise slowly and eventually she would get over her fear.

Before going into the house for the night, Amy put an old saddle in the palomino's stall. As she walked in with the saddle over her arm, Promise shied away, flattening her ears and throwing her head in the air.

"It's OK," Amy said, dropping the saddle to the floor. "I'm not going to put it on you." She waited outside to see how long it would take Promise to leave the back of her stall.

To her surprise, before she had even bolted the door Promise had walked over to the saddle and was sniffing it curiously. Then, with apparent unconcern, Promise turned to her hay net and continued to munch her hay. She didn't seem bothered about the saddle being there at all.

Strange, Amy thought. Usually a horse took quite a time getting used to whatever object it was that scared them. Apart from when Amy had been carrying the saddle, Promise had shown no hint of fear or unease at all. She guessed the valerian might have kicked in. But to have such a change, quite so soon? It wasn't normal. Feeling confused, Amy went into the farmhouse.

Lou and Marnie were sitting at the kitchen table, talking and poring over a page of figures. Their faces were serious.

"Hi!" Amy said.

"Hi!" Lou said briefly.

Marnie smiled quickly at Amy and then turned back to the papers and continued the conversation. "There must be something that can be done."

"What are you talking about?" Amy said, looking over their shoulders.

Lou shuffled the papers together. "Nothing."

Amy looked from one to the other. "What's going on?"

Marnie sighed. "You'd better tell her, Lou."

"It's OK," Lou said quickly to Amy. "Just some financial worries."

"Oh," Amy said, feeling slightly relieved that it wasn't anything serious. They always had financial worries. She fetched the biscuit jar and took out a couple of cookies. She turned and found Lou looking at her.

"You're not bothered, are you?" Lou said slowly.

Amy shrugged. "We always have money problems. We'll manage. We always do."

"Amy! Get real!" Frustration showed clearly on Lou's face. Marnie put a hand on her friend's arm but she brushed it off. "Things have never been this bad before! We've got bills we can't pay, no sources of credit, and no clients!"

"We've got Promise," Amy retorted.

"One horse?" Lou shook her head. "Amy! We can't run this place on the livery fees from one horse!"

"So what are you saying?" Amy demanded. "We just give up?"

Lou's response was swift. "We may have to."

Her words hung in the air.

"What?" Amy said, her insides feeling like she was falling from a great height.

Lou put her head in her hands. "I didn't want to tell you," she said hopelessly. "I know how worried you've been about Pegasus and how pleased you were to get Promise, but yes, unless we get some new clients in the immediate future, Heartland cannot carry on."

"No!" Amy stammered.

There was a horrible silence.

Marnie looked at her. "Lou and I have been trying to think of something, looking over the figures, looking at the assets. But she's right, Amy. It's not a good situation."

Amy took a step back, horrified. "It can't be true. What about the brochure and the advertising?"

"They haven't brought us any new business yet." Lou stood up and took her hand. "We're going to have to hope things get better, and fast, or the truth is we'll have to close this place down."

Chapter Eight

Amy hardly slept that night. She tossed and turned, thinking over what Lou had said. Heartland couldn't close! There had to be something they could do to keep it open. At five-thirty she gave up trying to sleep, and pulling on her jeans she went outside.

The early light was pale and the only sounds were the birds singing in the trees. Feeling sick with worry, Amy carried a saddle up to the circular training ring and then fetched Promise's halter. The only plan that she had been able to come up with was to cure Promise as quickly as possible in the hope that Lisa Stillman would send them some more horses.

Amy led the palomino up to the ring and went through the process of joining-up again. As the sun rose and the light brightened she tried putting a saddle on the palomino's back, but as soon as she had lifted the saddle off the gate the mare reared and fought. Eventually Amy gave up and took Promise back to her stall.

Before returning the halter to the tack-room, Amy looked over Pegasus' door. He was lying down, his muzzle resting on the straw, his breathing laboured. "Pegasus?" she said in alarm.

Pegasus staggered to his feet. His ribs were sticking out and the hollows in his sides moved in and out as he breathed. Amy went into his stall and checked him over. His breathing seemed to steady a bit, but he still didn't look well. Putting an arm over his back, Amy laid her face against the swell of his shoulders and felt tears well in her eyes. What else could she do?

"Amy?"

She jumped and swung round. Ty had arrived and was leaning on the half-door. "You OK?" he asked in concern.

"Yeah," she said quickly, brushing her eyes with her hand. "I'm fine." But as she met Ty's concerned look a sob leapt into her throat. "I don't know what to do, Ty," she burst out helplessly. "I've tried everything. Nothing's working." She looked at him desperately. "What else I can try?"

"I don't know," Ty said.

"There must be something!" Amy said in frustration. "Mom would have thought of something!"

She saw a muscle in Ty's jaw tighten.

"If only she was here!" Amy cried.

Ty nodded. "If only," he said quietly. With a sigh, he

straightened his shoulders. "Look, you stay here. I'll go and start on the feeds."

Amy watched him leave and, burying her face in Pegasus' mane, fought back her tears.

As Amy walked down the drive to catch the school bus, a turmoil of thoughts ran through her head – Pegasus, Promise, Heartland's future. As she walked past Pegasus' empty field she felt overwhelmed with sickness.

On the bus, she hardly said a word. Soraya and Matt seemed to sense that she didn't want to talk and left her alone. Several times she caught them exchanging worried looks.

"I'll see you guys later," Matt said quickly as they got off the bus. "I – I need to check the soccer fixture-list." Shooting a look at Soraya, he hurried away.

"So what's up?" Soraya asked, as she and Amy walked to their lockers.

Amy didn't answer. She didn't know what to say or where to start.

"Is it Pegasus?" Soraya asked.

"Yes. Well, partly," Amy said. She hugged her rucksack to her chest. "He's worse."

"Oh Amy, I'm so sorry," Soraya said, her eyes filling with sympathy.

"Nothing I do seems to make a difference," Amy said. "I just can't seem to cure him."

"Like that's surprising," Ashley's voice drawled.

Amy swung round. Ashley was standing behind her with Sherilyn.

"So the healing hands aren't working then?" Ashley said mockingly, her green eyes dancing at Amy's discomfort. Sherilyn smirked. "A healer who can't even heal her own horse! Now, *there's* a novelty."

"Give it a break, Ashley," Soraya snapped, unusually forceful. She put her hand on Amy's arm. "Come on, Amy, let's go."

Feeling too drained to cope with Ashley's taunts, Amy turned away.

"When are you going to face it, Amy?" Ashley called after her. "You and your sister are never going to make Heartland work without your mom."

Amy stiffened, but just as she was about to retaliate she was struck by the realization that Ashley's words might be true.

"Come *on!*" Soraya hissed, pulling her arm.

Amy followed Soraya dumbly. For the first time in her life, she was doubting herself and her own abilities. *Maybe I'm not good enough to carry on Heartland's work without Mom*, she thought. *After all, I haven't made any real progress with Promise and Pegasus is getting worse.* She felt sick again. Were Ashley's words going to come true?

By the time Amy got home from school she was feeling

intensely depressed. As she started the long walk up the drive, instead of the leap that her heart normally gave at being home again, she felt it sink at the thought of all the problems awaiting her.

To her surprise, as she reached the house the back door flew open. "Amy!" Lou said, her eyes shining. "We've been waiting for you to get home! Marnie and I have had an idea!"

"An idea?" Amy echoed, following her into the kitchen.

Marnie was standing by the sink. "A way of getting new customers for Heartland," she said, excitement lighting up her face.

Amy's hopes leapt. "What is it?"

"We organize an open day," Lou declared. "Not just one where people come and look round, but one where we actually show them what we do. You could demonstrate joining-up with a horse and Ty could explain the treatments we use — you know, the aromatherapy and the herbs and the—"

"I'm not doing it!" Amy exclaimed.

Lou stared at her. "Why not? It would be bound to get us customers. Most of them have never seen a join-up demonstration before — it's a magical experience!"

Amy shook her head desperately. After Ashley's words that afternoon the last thing she wanted was people coming out to Heartland. What would she say if they asked her about Promise? What would they think when they saw Pegasus?

Ashley's words echoed round and round in her head. Who would want to send their horse to a place that couldn't cure its own horse?

"But Amy," Lou said, looking at her in surprise, "don't you see? This could be the answer to our problems."

"Lou's right, Amy," Marnie said. "I'm sure if people actually saw how you worked they would be really keen to send problem horses here."

"I'm not doing it," Amy said firmly.

"But—" Lou began.

"No," Amy said.

Lou's temper suddenly seemed to snap. "Oh, for goodness' sake, Amy, grow up!" she shouted angrily, banging her fists down on the table. "Don't you realize that this is our last chance? You can't just say no!"

"I can't do it, Lou!" Amy shouted back. "Please don't ask me!" Flinging her rucksack down, she ran out of the house.

She didn't stop running until she reached Pegasus' stall. "Oh Pegasus!" she sobbed, going in and throwing her arms around his neck. "What are we going to do?" Burying her face in his mane, she breathed in his sweet smell and wished that everything could be different.

A few minutes later there was a slight cough behind her. "Amy?"

She turned. Marnie was standing in the doorway.

Pegasus whickered softly. Ever since the evening when Marnie had been wearing Marion's coat, he seemed to have taken a liking to her. He stretched out his nose. "Hi, big fella," Marnie said, stroking him.

Amy swallowed her tears.

"Um…" Marnie said hesitantly, "Lou's a bit upset, Amy."

Amy didn't say anything.

"The open day is a really good idea," Marnie said. "Why don't you want to do it?"

Amy looked at Pegasus. His ribs were standing out, his white coat looked stark and dull. "How can we have people here," she said hopelessly, "when I can't even cure Pegasus — my own horse?" A lump of tears swelled painfully in her throat. "It's no good," she said, shaking her head. "I'm no good."

Marnie looked at her in genuine astonishment. "But that's crazy! Lou's told me about all the horses you've cured — that little Shetland, and Nick Halliwell's horse, and the horse that was in the accident."

"But I'm not Mom," Amy whispered, hot tears welling in her eyes. "She would have cured Pegasus. She would have known what to do with Promise."

Marnie's blue eyes searched Amy's face. "But your mom had years and years of experience. Do you think she got it right all the time when she was learning? She would have made mistakes, had failures. But she didn't let that stop her." She took Amy's arm. "Anyway, for all you know, Pegasus could have a serious illness — something that even your mom wouldn't have been able to cure."

Amy bit her lip.

"Amy," Marnie said softly, "stop being so hard on yourself. You can't be your mom. All you can do is be yourself and listen to your own instincts."

"Mom used to say that," Amy whispered. "She always used to say that I had to trust my instincts."

"So do it!" Marnie said. "Look, Heartland can be a success, I'm sure of it. But only if you run it in your own way and for your own reasons, and only if you and Lou work together as a team. You've both got your own unique talents. You're great with the horses and Lou knows what she's doing with the books and business side of things. You have to find a way to use those talents together so that Heartland can thrive."

Slowly, Amy nodded and then took a deep breath. "I'll — I'll think about the open day."

Marnie smiled. "Good. I really think it could work." She squeezed Amy's arm. "And remember what your mom said — trust your instincts."

Amy watched her leave the stall. *Trust my instincts*.

"Promise!" she whispered, as the truth hit her. She had been so busy thinking about what Mom would have done that she had forgotten about listening to her own instincts. Not only that, she had also forgotten her mother's absolute rule — *listen to the horse*.

That evening, when the last of the work had been done and

Ty had left, Amy led Promise up to the circular schooling ring. Following the pattern of her previous sessions with the horse, she joined-up with her and then picked up the saddle from the gate. However, this time as Promise reared and struck out, Amy watched her eyes.

There was definitely no fear.

Dropping the saddle, Amy quickly moved Promise away, talking to her and leading her round until she was calm again. Then she stopped and thought.

At the sight of the saddle coming near her, Promise's eyes had filled with anger and – Amy struggled to find the right word – *resentment*. Yes, Promise had looked resentful.

For a moment, Amy looked at the horse. *Why?* She thought about everything she had heard about Promise. As she remembered the details of Promise's life prior to belonging to Lisa Stillman, Amy suddenly had a hunch that she was close to finding what was at the root of the problem.

Unclipping the long-line, she set Promise loose in the empty field next to the training ring and secured the gate before hurrying down the yard to the kitchen. To her relief, Lou and Marnie were upstairs. She picked up the phone.

A quick call to Scott gave her the telephone number that she wanted. She punched the numbers in and waited, still not sure exactly what it was that she was trying to find out.

The phone was picked up. A woman who sounded about seventy answered. "Eliza Chittick speaking," she said briskly.

"Hi!" Amy said. "This is Amy Fleming from Heartland

Equine Sanctuary. I have a horse you bred — Promise, a palomino. I'm working on her for Lisa Stillman, and I was wondering if you could help me with some details about her background."

"Promise?" Mrs Chittick said, her voice immediately softening. "Why, sure I can help. Fire away."

Amy explained about Promise's aversion to tack.

"I'd heard from Lisa she was being difficult," Mrs Chittick said, sounding worried, "but I had no idea it was this bad. She was perfect when she was here. A horse in a million. Did Lisa tell you that my grandson used to ride her? He's almost totally blind and she was as gentle as a lamb with him."

"She did mention it," Amy said, still not quite sure what information she was after from Mrs Chittick but feeling sure that the key to Promise's behaviour somehow lay in her past. "Was she good with him?"

"Wonderful," Mrs Chittick said. "We trusted her completely. She was his eyes. She would take him places and bring him back. He'd ride her bareback with just a halter. I've never known a more intelligent horse. More human than horse really." Amy heard her smile. "And I guess that's how we treated her. Somehow, when you were doing things with her, you almost felt that you had to ask her permission."

Something in Amy's brain suddenly seemed to click into place. *That was it!* Her fingers gripped the receiver in excitement. She was sure that she had got it.

"Like I said, she was a horse in a million," Mrs Chittick

continued. "I just can't believe that Lisa's having these problems with her. The horses are treated well at Fairfield — big barns, lots of stable-hands, the best of care. I can't understand what's gone wrong."

Amy thanked Mrs Chittick for the information and promised to ring her with news on Promise's progress. Putting the receiver down she leant against the wall. Yes, at Fairfield the horses were undoubtedly treated well — but they were treated like horses. And that wasn't what Promise had been used to.

Amy hurried back to the field. Promise was grazing in the fading light, but as Amy undid the gate she walked over, her head outstretched, her delicate ears pricked. Amy rubbed her forehead and tried to imagine what it must have been like for Promise. All her life she had been treated as an individual, trusted, respected and loved, and then suddenly she had been uprooted from everything she knew and placed in a yard where she was treated like any other horse.

Amy remembered what Lisa Stillman had said about the first day that Promise had been tacked up. She could picture it only too well. The tack arriving and being thrown swiftly on to Promise's back. Promise objecting to what she saw as rough handling and being slapped by the stable-hand, and retaliating by biting and being punished further.

Amy studied Promise's head — confident, intelligent, bold. Whereas most horses would have submitted to the discipline, Promise had chosen to fight the firm handling with aggression. The stronger people got with her, the more aggressive she had become. Arabians were a proud breed and every line of Promise's body, every contour of her head suggested that she had that pride in bucket-loads. She was a horse that would never submit.

"And yet I wasn't strong with you," Amy whispered to the golden horse. "So why fight me?"

Think horse, she said to herself. She looked at the saddle and imagined it from Promise's point of view. After the first time when she had kicked out at the stable-hand, the staff at Fairfield would have approached saddling her with firm words and ready slaps, and a confrontation would have ensued. Now the sight of someone carrying a saddle was enough to make Promise go wild. Joining-up, although powerful, had not been enough to show Promise that she was respected and trusted. Somehow she had to break the negative association with the saddle.

So what do I do? Amy thought.

She stood for a moment, looking at the horse, and all of a sudden she knew. She clipped the long-line on to Promise's halter and stroked the mare's neck before her hands moved experimentally to press on the mare's back.

Promise turned and looked at her.

"May I?" Amy whispered.

Promise turned her head back to face forward. Taking a deep breath, Amy grasped the long creamy mane and vaulted on to Promise's back. As she landed she tensed, half expecting her theory to be wrong and the mare to explode – but nothing happened. Promise stood still and steady.

Amy relaxed. "Walk on," she said, squeezing with her legs. Promise moved forward, her body warm under Amy's legs.

Amy guided her around the field, using the halter and pressure from her knees. Promise seemed calm and happy, striding out, her action smooth and effortless, her ears pricked. After a few circuits Amy asked the mare to trot. Her stride was bouncy, but Amy relaxed into it, letting her body absorb the movement.

She stroked Promise's neck. She couldn't resist it – leaning forward she urged the mare into a canter. Promise leapt forward, her ears pricked. Amy grasped the mane, her body forward, her eyes alight. She could feel the power surging through Promise's muscles, feel her quarters gather and push.

"Faster!" she whispered.

With a surge, Promise's stride lengthened. Her mane whipped back into Amy's face, the wind dragging tears from Amy's eyes. Bending low over her neck, Amy lost herself in the thunder of hooves and the power and speed of the golden horse beneath her.

At long last she slowed Promise down, easing her to a trot, a walk and finally to a halt. Leaning forward she kissed Promise's neck and then slid off. Promise nuzzled Amy's shoulder and then, lifting her muzzle to Amy's face, blew in and out. For the first time since she had come to Heartland, her eyes looked genuinely happy.

"Now let's see about the saddle," Amy said. She hitched Promise to the fence and fetched the saddle from the schooling ring. Walking back through the gate she watched Promise's reaction carefully. Promise turned and looked, but did nothing else. Amy could feel her heart speeding up in her chest. She approached the horse. She reached Promise's side.

"May I?" Amy asked, offering the saddle to the mare. Promise snorted at the saddle but did not move.

Holding her breath, Amy lifted it up and gently slid it on to the mare's back. Promise stayed still.

Fingers trembling, Amy did up the girth. The saddle was on. She pulled down the stirrups and, not bothering with a bridle, mounted.

Nothing happened.

Amy stroked Promise's neck in delight. "Walk on."

After several times around the field, Amy halted Promise by the gate. Dusk had fallen, but Amy was so elated that she hardly noticed. Promise had allowed herself to be saddled and ridden! She knew that it wasn't enough for Promise just to let one person saddle and ride her, but that could be worked on. Amy dismounted and hugged the mare.

The breakthrough had been made.

Chapter Nine

The following morning, Amy woke early again and hurried out of the house. If she was quick she would have time to work Promise before school. She hadn't told Lou and Marnie of her success the night before. It had all felt somehow unreal, and she decided to ride Promise one more time before she told anyone.

The palomino was looking out over her stall door. She whinnied softly when she saw Amy, her eyes shining. Amy felt a warm glow of happiness. Suddenly she just knew that Promise was going to be OK.

She fetched the mare's halter, but before returning went to check over Pegasus' door.

Her heart stopped.

Pegasus was lying on his side, his head and neck stretched out in the straw. For an awful moment Amy thought he was dead, but then she saw his side rise and fall.

Dropping the halter, she fumbled with the bolt and ran into his stall. "Pegasus?" she gasped.

The great horse lifted his head slightly. His nostrils quivered in a faint whicker and then his head fell to the straw again.

Icy fingers clutched at Amy's heart. She stood undecided for a moment and then turned and raced down to the house. "Lou!" she screamed, flinging the door open. "Lou! Quick!"

A few seconds later, Lou came stumbling into the kitchen, her eyes blinking, her hair sticking up. "Amy, whatever's the matter? It's only six o'clock."

"It's Pegasus!" The words left Amy in gasps. "He's down in his stall. I don't think he's going to get up again."

The sleepiness left Lou's face in an instant. "I'll ring Scott. You go back to him. I'll be out as soon as I'm dressed."

Amy ran back to Pegasus' stall. He was lying there, motionless. Amy knelt down by his head. His eyelids flickered, and lifting his head slightly he rested his muzzle against her knees. He groaned quietly. Bending over, Amy cradled his huge head in her arms, kissing his ears, his eyelids, the soft skin above his nostrils. Her fingers stroked him frantically. "It's OK, boy," she said. "It's going to be OK." She repeated the words over and over again, desperate to believe them, to somehow make them true. But deep down she knew the awful truth. It was finally the end – Pegasus was dying.

There was the sound of running footsteps. Marnie appeared in the stall doorway. "Lou's speaking to Scott now."

At the sound of her voice, Pegasus lifted his head and for one brief second his eyes seemed to brighten. But then he sighed and his head sank to the ground again.

"Is there anything I can get you?" Marnie said to Amy.

Amy shook her head, tears blurring her eyes. "I don't think so." Looking at Pegasus' side, she saw that his breathing was getting shallower. She stroked his cheek. His half-closed eyes were dull. It was as if the spark inside him that had started to fade when Marion had died had finally gone out. Amy suddenly looked at Marnie. "The coat!" she said.

"Which coat?" Then Marnie's eyes suddenly widened with realization. "You mean your mom's barn-jacket?"

"Yes," Amy said quickly. "Where is it?"

"In my room."

"Can you get it, please?" Amy whispered. "I think it might help."

Marnie hurried down the yard.

Amy stroked Pegasus' head. "There, boy, it's going to be just fine. You'll see."

Lou arrived at the stall. "Scott's on his way," she said. She knelt down beside Pegasus. "Hey, boy," she said softly.

Just then, Marnie came back with the jacket. "What do you want me to do with it?"

"Can I have it?" Amy said. As she reached for it, Pegasus caught its scent. Lifting his head he whinnied hoarsely and, making a great effort, reached towards the jacket. All three of them said nothing, their eyes fixed on his face.

Pegasus breathed in and out for a long moment.

Then, seeing his head about to fall, Amy folded the jacket on to her knee and guided it gently down. Blinking back the tears, she stroked his face as he nuzzled the worn fabric. He looked happier, but the effort he had made had been too much for him. His breathing grew shallower. And then his eyes closed and he sighed, his head sliding off her lap and sinking to the ground.

Amy started to sob. "Please don't die, Pegasus! *Please!*"

Lou put an arm around her shoulders. "His body is old," she said softly. "His heart is broken. We have to let him go."

Just then there was the sound of footsteps coming up to the stall. Amy glanced round. It was Scott. One look at his face was enough.

"There's nothing we can do, is there?" Amy sobbed.

Scott shook his head sadly as he looked at the horse. "Amy, you've given him a wonderful home, an ideal life. But life doesn't last for ever."

"But Mom – Mom would want us to try," Amy cried in anguish.

"Your mom would understand, Amy," Scott said as he crouched down beside her and ran his hand over Pegasus' shoulder and chest. "I didn't want to worry you, but you see these swellings?" he said, pointing out a number of fluid-filled lumps on the underside of Pegasus' chest. Amy nodded. She had noticed them before but had thought they were just an allergic reaction to fly bites. "They suggest he has some form of internal tumour, a lymphosarcoma I'd guess," Scott told her.

"A tumour — *cancer*?" Amy stammered.

Scott nodded. "I suspected it last time I saw him." His eyes sought hers. "And the last batch of tests came back late last night. They were positive. Amy, there isn't anything we can do to cure him. Some diseases simply can't be healed." He paused. "We can't let him suffer, Amy," he said. "It simply isn't fair."

Amy bit hard on her lower lip, desperately struggling to hold back the sobs that were threatening to shake her body. Part of her wanted to cling on to every last moment she had with Pegasus. But Scott was right — she couldn't let him suffer any longer. However hard it was, she had to cope with the pain to help the horse she loved.

"Amy?" Scott said softly.

Amy looked up at him. She knew he was asking permission to put her dear old friend to sleep. With tears streaming down her face, she nodded slowly.

"It won't take long," Scott said, opening his black bag and taking out a needle. "He won't feel a thing. I promise."

For the last time, Amy bent her head to Pegasus'. His eyelids blinked. "I love you, Pegasus. I always will," she whispered, hot tears falling on his face. "Please understand, I'm doing this to help you."

She kissed his muzzle and then, sobbing bitterly, she cradled his head as Scott administered the injection.

Within a few long seconds, Pegasus' breathing had stopped.

"That's it," Scott said softly. "He's gone."

Amy gasped, staring at Pegasus in anguish.

"It was the right choice, Amy," Lou said. She put an arm around her. "The only choice. Now he'll be with Mom again."

In that moment, Amy suddenly realized how much she needed her sister. "Oh Lou," she sobbed against her shoulder, "I'm so glad you're here."

"And I always will be," Lou said intensely. "I'll always be here for you, Amy, and you'll be here for me. We need each other."

Amy pulled back, suddenly realizing how stupid it was to have pointless arguments. "We can have an open day if you like, Lou," she said. "I'll do whatever it takes. Heartland has to survive."

"It will, Amy," Lou said as their eyes met. "If we work together, it will!"

Chapter Ten

That night, Amy rang Grandpa to tell him about Pegasus. At first he wanted to return immediately.

"No, it's OK. Stay a bit longer," she told him.

"But I feel terrible," he protested. "I should have been there."

"There wasn't anything you could have done," Amy replied. "There was nothing anyone could have done." The tears gathered in her throat but she felt inwardly calm. She knew that she had done the right thing. Pegasus' suffering was over.

"And what about his body?"

"Scott and Ty dug a grave in his field," Amy said quietly. "And we planted an oak sapling beside it." She glanced out of the kitchen window. It was getting dark now but she could still make out the field and the slim young tree, silhouetted against the evening sky. "You don't have to come home early, Grandpa. We're managing."

"Well, I'll stay until next Sunday then, like I planned," Grandpa said. "But if you need me, promise you'll ring."

"I promise."

Just then Lou came into the kitchen. "Is that Grandpa?" she asked.

Amy nodded. "Here's Lou, Grandpa," she said, handing over the phone.

As Lou spoke to Grandpa, telling him about the open day they were planning, Amy leant against the sink and stared out at Pegasus' tree. She found it almost impossible to believe that he wasn't in his stall and that when she went out to feed the horses the next morning he wouldn't be there. But looking up at the grey sky she knew that she had to accept it: Pegasus was gone and life had to move on.

"It's all settled then," Lou said, putting the phone down. "We're going to have the open day next Sunday – Marnie's last day. Grandpa thinks it's a great idea." She looked at Amy. "You know, I think this is going to be one busy week."

Lou was right. There was a lot to be done: posters to be designed, adverts to be placed, catering to be sorted out, road signs to be put up and the final smartening touches made to the stables. Marnie, Soraya and Matt all helped as much as they could, and Amy found the days passing in a whirl of activity – going to school, helping with the open day preparations, doing her normal chores, working Promise in the mornings and evenings. At night, when she fell into her bed, she was too exhausted to think and brood, too tired even to dream.

The next Thursday, Scott dropped by. Amy was sweeping the yard with Ty, Marnie was deadheading the flowers in the hanging baskets and Lou was attaching the nameplates to the horses' doors.

"Hi there!" Scott called, easing his broad-shouldered frame out of the car. "I just thought I'd stop by and see how you're getting on."

"We're doing fine," Lou said, going down the yard to meet him, screwdriver in hand. "Almost ready for the big day."

"I've been spreading the word," Scott said, "so I hope you're expecting a big crowd."

"That's the plan," Lou said.

They stopped a few steps away from each other. "So how are you?" Lou asked, her cheeks flushing slightly pink.

Amy and Marnie exchanged knowing looks.

"Fine," Scott replied to Lou. "Listen, do you need any help on Sunday? I'm happy to lend a hand."

"Thanks," Lou said. "That would be really great." She smiled up at him.

There was a pause as they looked at each other. Suddenly seeming to become aware that they were being watched, Scott cleared his throat and turned to Amy. "So ... how's it going with Promise?" he asked. "Have you made any progress?"

"You bet she has!" Ty said, leaning on his broom. "This girl's amazing!"

"She's letting you get the tack near her?" Scott said to Amy.

Amy grinned at him. "Why don't you come and see."

Fetching Promise's halter, Amy led the palomino to the training ring on a long-line, the saddle and bridle over her arm.

"So what have you been doing with her?" Scott asked, opening the gate for her. "Lunging? Long-reining?"

"Riding," Amy replied, leading Promise into the ring. She grinned at his astonished face. "Watch."

She patted Promise and then vaulted lightly on to her back. After riding the mare several times around the school, she halted.

"That's great," Scott said, looking impressed. He glanced at the tack. "What about the saddle and bridle?"

"Oh, I can ride with those as well," Amy said. Her voice was casual but inwardly she was fizzing with delight. She couldn't wait to see Scott's face!

Swinging her leg over Promise's back, she dismounted and fetched the saddle. She offered it to Promise to sniff and then, when Promise had turned away, lifted it carefully on to the mare's golden back. The horse stood without moving as Amy did up the girth and then slipped on the bridle. Putting her foot in the stirrup, she mounted and rode round in a circle.

"Well," she said, stopping Promise by the gate, as the sweet sensation of success flowed through her, "what do you think?"

"She's like a different horse!" Scott exclaimed. He ran a hand through his hair. "Just how did you do it?"

"By listening," Amy said simply, "and respecting her."

"And she's OK for other people to ride?" Scott asked.

"She's getting there," Amy said. Only the day before, Promise had let Ty tack her up and ride her. She was still a little sensitive about the saddle being lifted near her, but with careful handling, Amy was sure that it would pass.

"No one's going to believe this," Scott said, shaking his head. "Have you told Lisa yet?"

"I was going to ring her tonight," Amy said.

"She'll be over the moon," Scott said. His blue eyes looked suddenly thoughtful. "You know, you should ask her permission to use Promise at the open day. People round here have heard of her. If they see that you've cured a supposedly rogue horse like that, they're bound to be impressed."

Amy thought for a moment. Why not? She knew Lou wanted her to do a display of joining-up with a horse for the visitors to see. Why not use Promise if Lisa Stillman agreed? After all, it would have an impact on people who had heard about the palomino and for those who hadn't – well, she was a very pretty, healthy horse and would look good in a display. The question was, would Lisa Stillman give her the go-ahead?

After Scott had left, Amy phoned Fairfield. Lisa Stillman sounded astonished to hear that Promise was already ridable. "But you've only had her just over a week!" she said. "And you're telling me she's cured?"

"Well, not completely," Amy replied, "but she's definitely improving. I can ride her and saddle her up no problem. I just want her to get more confident with other people."

"But other stables had her for months at a time and not one of them ever made a difference," Lisa Stillman said. "How on earth have you done it?"

Amy explained about her phone-call to Eliza Chittick and about how Promise's behaviour had changed when she had started trusting her and treating her like an intelligent being.

"This is amazing!" Lisa Stillman said, as she listened to Amy's tale. "I have to see her!"

"Well, I was ringing to ask you if we could use Promise in a demonstration next Sunday. We're having an open day at Heartland." Amy explained about the idea behind the open day and how she needed a horse to join-up with. "Promise would be ideal – if you'll give your permission, of course," she added politely.

"Sure you can use her," Lisa Stillman said. "I'll even come along myself to see what you've been doing. What time does it start?"

"Eleven o'clock," Amy said, "and the demonstration will be at twelve."

"I'll see you then," Lisa Stillman said.

Amy put the phone down, feeling excited but nervous. She knew that Ty was carefully preparing his talk about the alternative remedies they used at Heartland. His bit of the demonstration was bound to go well. But the join-up? It was normally such a private, intense experience. How would she feel doing it in front of a whole load of strangers? What if it didn't work?

She pushed such thoughts away. It had to work. After all, Heartland's future depended upon the demonstration being a success. And she would do anything to keep Heartland going. She had made a promise to Mom.

The final few days before the open day seemed to race by, but by a quarter to eleven on Sunday morning Heartland was finally ready for the visitors to arrive. Amy, Lou, Marnie, Ty and Soraya stood in the middle of the yard.

"We're done!" Lou said, looking round in relief.

"And it's looking good!" Marnie said, gazing round at the front stable block and the spotless yard.

"It sure is," Amy agreed. She looked at the horses who had their heads over their stall doors, their coats gleaming and their eyes shining with health. The hanging baskets provided a splash of cheerful colour against the dark wood of the stables. Around the yard, Ty had put up signs to show visitors where to go. "It all looks so tidy and clean!" she exclaimed.

"Unlike you!" Ty grinned.

Amy looked down at her filthy jeans. She had started work at five-thirty that morning and hadn't had a second even to brush her hair. "I guess I'd better get changed," she admitted.

"Me too," said Soraya.

They hurried upstairs to Amy's bedroom and changed into breeches and clean T-shirts. "I hope everything goes OK," Amy said, feeling butterflies starting to flutter in her stomach.

"It will," Soraya said, pulling her dark curls back into a neat pony-tail. She glanced out of the window. "We'd better hurry! I think the first people are arriving!"

They raced downstairs to find Ty directing a car-load of visitors into the field they were using as a temporary car park. Just then, Scott's car came up the drive. He stopped it outside the house and he and Matt jumped out.

"Hi, there!" Lou said, coming out of the house with a box of Cokes for the drinks and refreshments stall that Marnie was looking after.

"Sorry we're late," Scott said. "I was called out first thing." He saw her struggling and strode over. "Hey, do you want a hand?"

"Thanks," Lou said gratefully, letting him take the box from her. "There's a couple more boxes inside."

"No problem," Scott said smiling down at her. "Just think of me as your slave."

Lou raised her eyebrows. "That sounds fun."

They both laughed and walked off towards the drinks table.

"Hey, guys," Matt said, going over to Amy and Soraya. "What do you want me to do?"

"Could you take over the parking from Ty?" Amy suggested. "Soraya and I are going to show people round and Ty's supposed to be giving out brochures and talking about what we do here."

"Sure. No problem," said Matt, loping off.

The first group of visitors headed towards the yard. Soraya glanced at Amy. "Well, here we go," she muttered as the visitors drew closer. "Get ready to smile."

Amy nodded and, taking a deep breath, stepped forward. "Hi!" she said brightly. "I'm Amy Fleming. Welcome to Heartland."

Soon the place was teeming with people. Although most of them were really friendly and interested in Heartland's work, there were some who clearly doubted the effectiveness of the methods used. Amy struggled to keep control of her temper.

"If one more person tells me that aromatherapy or herbal remedies don't work with horses, then I'm going to scream," she muttered to Ty as she stopped to collect some brochures from him.

Further up the yard she could see Soraya telling a group of visitors the history of each horse.

"Relax," Ty said to her. He shrugged. "Not everyone here's prepared to be converted. We have to accept that. The day will be a success if we get just a few of them interested enough in our methods to think about sending their problem horses here."

But Amy couldn't think like that. She knew the methods they used at Heartland worked and she desperately wanted *all* the visitors to realize that – to see what a unique and special place it really was.

"But why have they come if they're not prepared to listen?" she demanded, thinking of the last man she had talked to and his refusal to believe that any alternative remedies could have an effect. "They just seem to want to criticize."

"Yeah," Ty said easily. His eyes suddenly fixed on a point behind Amy's shoulder. "Talking of which…"

Amy swung round. Ashley Grant was sauntering up the yard. Beside her was her mom – a thick-set woman with short blonde hair.

"What are they doing here?" Amy hissed.

Val Grant caught sight of her and came over. "Hello, Amy," she said, her smile revealing a mouthful of perfect white teeth. "We thought we'd pop by and offer you our support."

Like that's true, Amy thought to herself. But she forced herself to smile back. "It's nice to see you."

Val Grant's eyes flashed round. "You've sure straightened this place out a bit."

"Hi, Ty," Ashley said, virtually ignoring Amy. She flicked her hair back. "How are you?"

"Fine." Ty coughed and started to shuffle the brochures.

"They look good," Ashley said. She leant forward to look through one and her shoulder brushed against his. Amy saw her glance sideways at him and smile.

Feeling a wave of irritation she turned to excuse herself. "I'd better be going," she said to Val Grant. "There are people to see."

"Sure thing," Val Grant said. "We'll just have a look round. We're looking forward to seeing the demonstration later." She laughed. At least her mouth did, but her eyes stayed hard. "You never know, we may learn something."

Amy smiled briefly and then hurried away. Now, more than ever, she was determined that the join-up would succeed.

At twelve o'clock, Scott, Lou and Marnie started to encourage people to go to the schooling ring. Amy put Promise's saddle and bridle on the fence and then went to fetch the palomino.

"This is it, girl," she said, rubbing Promise's golden neck. "Please be good." Suddenly she realized that she hadn't seen Lisa Stillman. She felt a flash of disappointment but quickly pushed it down. There were more than enough people out there to impress.

She led Promise up to the training ring. At the sight of the people clustered two deep around the fence, her stomach knotted with fear.

Ty had already started his talk.

To demonstrate the use of aromatherapy oils, Soraya led Sugarfoot into the ring and Ty showed the crowd how the Shetland turned away from certain oils but sniffed long and hard at two of the bottles. "Horses appear instinctively to know what will help them," he told the crowd. "When Sugarfoot first came to Heartland after his owner died, he showed a preference for neroli oil – an oil used for dealing with grief and the loss of the will to recover. However, now that he is recovering, he is showing his preference for bergamot and yarrow oils. Bergamot is a balancing and uplifting oil, while yarrow relaxes. Sugarfoot is instinctively choosing the oils that will help him most effectively at this time."

Ty then started to work on the Shetland with T-Touch circles, and again pointed out to the audience how the Shetland moved himself to place certain parts of his head and body under his fingers.

Amy noticed the growing interest of the crowd as they began to murmur to one another.

"He's telling me how to help him," Ty told them. Leaving Sugarfoot, he walked round the ring. "Horses try and communicate with us, but time after time they find that humans just don't listen," he said. He looked around, his dark eyes fired with passion. "Well, at Heartland we believe in listening. We don't whisper things to the horses, we let *them* speak to *us*."

As he finished there was a burst of applause.

Promise started at the sudden noise. "It's OK," Amy soothed her quickly.

Soraya led Sugarfoot out of the ring and Ty held up his hand for quiet. "We'd now like to show you another way that we listen to the horse. It's called join-up." He led a further round of applause and then walked over to the gate where Amy was waiting. He opened the gate. "Over to you," he said to Amy. "Good luck."

Their eyes met and Ty squeezed her shoulder. "Go on," he said. "I know you can do it."

Taking a deep breath, Amy braced herself and led Promise into the ring.

The clapping died down and an expectant hush descended.

Horribly aware of the eyes watching her, Amy unclipped the lead-rope and let Promise go. As the palomino trotted off round the ring, Amy heard a few murmurs and gasps from the people in the crowd who recognized her as Lisa Stillman's rogue horse. Amy knew she had to speak, to explain what she was doing, but for a moment her courage failed her. Suddenly she caught sight of Lou in the crowd. Her sister smiled encouragingly at her and Amy felt her confidence return.

"Promise is a horse who came to us with a behaviour problem," she told the crowd. "For months she had been considered virtually unridable. And then she came to

Heartland. She has been here for two weeks and her problem is pretty much cured – as I will show you at the end of this demonstration," she said, motioning to the saddle and bridle on the fence. "But first of all I will show you the technique we use to establish a relationship with a horse. Not a traditional relationship based on fear, but a relationship based on trust and understanding."

Moving to the centre of the ring, she began.

The join-up worked like a dream. Amy explained every signal that Promise gave to the audience. She felt their collective tension when she dropped her eyes and turned her back on the mare, heard the universal intake of breath as Promise walked confidently over to her and rested her muzzle on Amy's shoulder, and sensed their astonishment as she walked around the ring with the palomino following wherever she went.

To end the demonstration, Amy picked up the saddle and offered it to Promise. "I'm asking her whether I can saddle her up," she told the crowd. "By asking her per-mission I am showing that I respect her. Promise is a highly intelligent, proud horse – too proud to be bullied into obedience."

After Promise had sniffed the saddle, Amy tacked her up, mounted, and then rode round the ring. She trotted the palomino in two serpentines and then cantered her in a perfect figure of eight.

Drawing Promise to a halt in the middle of the ring, she

dismounted. "In two weeks, this horse has changed from a rogue into the perfect riding horse." She smiled at the crowd. "And all because, here at Heartland, we listen to the horse."

The applause broke out. It went on and on. Patting Promise, Amy smiled happily. They had done it! She and Promise had shown them all!

Ty came back into the ring. "So, are there any questions?"

There was a murmur in the crowd and then a man raised his hand. It was the same man Amy had been talking to earlier, who seemed determined not to believe that Heartland's methods could work.

"How do we know that the horse really was unridable?" he demanded. "We only have your word for it."

"True," Ty replied. "But there are enough people here who know or who have heard of this horse to corroborate our claims."

Amy heard the crowd murmur an assent. There was a movement near the gate.

"It's my belief that horse is doped!" The voice was loud and strident. Amy swung round to see Val Grant pushing her way to the front of the fence. "It's the oldest trick in the book," the blonde woman announced. "Get a rogue horse, sedate it, and then make it look like you've worked a miracle. Mark my words, come here tomorrow and you'll see a very different animal."

To Amy's horror, people in the crowd started to nod.

"That's not true!" she exclaimed. "I'd never dope a horse."

"Well, of course you'd say that," the first man spoke up again. "You want our business."

"Not if it means doping a horse!" Amy said.

Val Grant spoke up again. "Sorry, honey, these people just don't seem to believe you."

"I believe you." The crowd turned. A woman pushed open the gate and walked into the ring. With her long blonde hair and elegant riding breeches, Lisa Stillman was instantly recognizable to all those who followed showing classes.

"Lisa!" Amy gasped.

Lisa Stillman walked to the centre of the ring. "What some of you may not realize," she drawled, "is that this horse is one of mine. I can vouch for the fact that she was as un-ridable as Amy Fleming says. Although," she shot a caustic look at the man who had spoken out and Val Grant, "you may of course choose to doubt my word as well." She looked round at the rest of the audience. "The fact is, it's true. This was the horse's last chance and as far as I'm concerned Heartland have worked nothing less than a miracle. She isn't doped – anyone can see that by taking a look at her eyes." She patted Promise. "When I first agreed to let Promise come here, I was as sceptical as many of you are," she announced. "But not any more. After what I've just seen, I realize that this is the way forward. From now on," Lisa turned and smiled at Amy, "any problem horse of mine will be coming to Heartland."

"Thank you!" Amy gasped.

"And now," Lisa Stillman said, "I think we should give our hosts a round of applause."

This time the applause was deafening. People clapped their hands, whistled and stamped their feet. Seeing Promise's startled expression, Amy quickly led her out of the ring and back to the peaceful sanctuary of her stall.

"Thank you," she whispered to the mare.

Promise snorted and nuzzled her shoulder.

Suddenly the stall door flew open. It was Matt and Soraya. "Wasn't that fantastic?" Soraya gasped.

"The way that Lisa Stillman woman just marched into the ring was so cool!" Matt laughed.

"Val Grant didn't know where to look!" Soraya grinned. "We've just seen her storming back to her car with Ashley, looking really mad." She hugged Amy. "And you were great! You seemed so cool and confident."

Amy grinned. "I was terrified!"

"You should see the chaos up by the ring now," Matt said. "Everyone's trying to talk to Lou and Ty about booking their horses in here. You're going to have an enormous waiting list."

Amy could hardly believe it, but when she returned to the ring with Soraya and Matt she was forced to admit they were right. People were simply crowding round Lou and Ty. Amy's eyes widened. It was wonderful, just what they'd wanted, but how were they ever going to cope with the extra work?

Her sister suddenly spotted her. "Amy!" she called, waving.

Amy made her way through the crowd with people patting her on the back and congratulating her. "Hi!" she exclaimed, reaching Lou. "Isn't this amazing?"

"Yeah," Lou said. "Look at this!" She waved a piece of paper filled with names and addresses under Amy's nose. "And Ty's collected more. After today we'll be able to fill the barns three times over."

"How will we cope?" Amy cried, half in delight, half in despair.

"That's the best bit ever," Lou said. "Lisa Stillman's asked if we'll take on her nephew Ben as a stable-hand. She wants him to learn everything we do so that in the end he can return to her stud and practise the same therapies we use, there. Even better – she's going to pay us to have him!"

"I just can't believe it, Lou!" Amy gasped, flinging her arms round her sister's neck. "This solves all our problems!"

Lou hugged her back joyfully.

"I know you said you'd have wild parties when I was gone," a familiar voice said behind them, "but isn't this a bit much?"

Amy and Lou turned. "Grandpa!" they both cried in delight.

Jack Bartlett smiled at them. "Yes," he said, "I'm home."

That evening, after the horses had been fed and the yard cleared, Amy walked down the drive to Pegasus' field. The air was still and peaceful. She leant over the wooden gate and watched the shadows lengthening across the grass.

Ty, Soraya, Matt and Scott had gone home and Marnie was in her bedroom, packing for her journey back to the city the next day. Amy knew she was going to miss her. After all, it was Marnie who had made her realize that she had to run Heartland in her own way and for her own reasons, but that she and Lou had to work together as a team.

A cool breeze shivered across Amy's skin. After the hubbub of the open day everything seemed doubly quiet. It had been a huge success. For the moment at least, Heartland's financial worries were over, and with Ben Stillman as an additional stable-hand there would be more time to spend with the horses. *Maybe I'll even get the chance to enter some jumping classes*, Amy thought.

She looked at the slender young oak tree and her heart twisted. Just one thing was missing from her life – Pegasus.

"Why did you have to go?" she whispered painfully.

But even as she spoke, she knew the answer. Life moved on. Nothing lasted for ever.

The light faded and the evening shadows covered the tree. A last, lone bird sang out.

"Amy?"

She looked round. Grandpa and Lou were walking towards her through the October dusk.

"We saw you from the kitchen window," Lou said.

"You don't mind us joining you, do you?" Grandpa asked quietly.

Amy shook her head.

For a moment all three of them stood by the gate in silence. "Today was a good day," Lou said at last.

Amy smiled. "Thanks to you, Lou. It was your idea."

Grandpa put a hand lightly on each of their shoulders. "I'm proud of both of you," he said, his voice full of emotion. "And your mom would have been proud of you too. You've made Heartland your own." He squeezed their shoulders. "You've found a way to build on the past and move on into the future."

"As a team," Amy said, glancing at Lou.

Lou smiled back. "Yes, as a team."

Amy looked towards the oak. Grandpa was right. Life was about the future, not clinging to the past. Staring at the tree, her lips moved silently. "*Goodbye, Pegasus.*"

Despite the shadows of the night, the bird sang on.

Read more about Amy's world at

Heartland™

in book four

Taking Chances

Amy finished filling up a water bucket and glanced at her watch. It was twelve-thirty. Soraya would be arriving any minute. She deposited the bucket in Solo's stall and went up to the top of the drive to wait for her friend.

On either side of the driveway, horses and ponies grazed contentedly in the turn-out paddocks, the October breeze ruffling their coats and sending the occasional red or gold leaf skittering across the short grass.

Only one paddock was empty. In the middle of it stood a single oak sapling, the soil still fresh around its base.

Amy walked over to the wooden gate. "Pegasus," she whispered, a wave of sadness flooding over her as she looked at the young tree. She could hardly believe it was really only three weeks since Pegasus had been buried there.

"Oh, Pegasus." Amy pictured the great grey horse.

In his younger days, he had been one of the most famous show-jumpers in the world. But Amy remembered him better as the horse who had let her play round his legs when she little, and who had nuzzled her when she was upset. To her, he was the horse whose strong presence had helped her through the nightmare of her mom being killed in a road accident four months ago, and the horse who had been her friend.

Amy swallowed as she looked at the sapling. *Everything's changed so much in the last few months*, she thought to herself. *Mom's gone. Pegasus's gone. Lou's come back*.

Lou's return to Heartland was one of the few good things

to have happened. Until recently, Amy's older sister had worked in Manhattan, but since their mom's death she had decided to leave her banking job and live permanently at Heartland — the equine sanctuary their mom, Marion, had set up on their grandpa's farm.

The sound of a car coming up the drive roused Amy from her thoughts. She looked round.

Soraya Martin, her best friend, was waving madly from the front passenger seat as her mom's car came up the drive. Amy took a deep breath, swallowing hard and pushing down the ache of painful memories. She waved back — forcing herself to smile, burying her inner sadness.

"Hi!" Soraya called, winding down the window. "Sorry I'm late. Mom had to pick up some groceries on the way over." The car drew to a halt and Soraya jumped out, black curls bouncing on her shoulders. "See you later, Mom," she said. "Thanks for the ride."

"Sure," Mrs Martin said, smiling at Amy. "Now, you girls have fun."

Amy and Soraya grinned at each other. "We will," they both said at once.

Half an hour later, Amy tightened her fingers on Sundance's reins and looked towards the fallen tree that lay across one side of the trail. "Come on then, boy," she whispered. "Let's jump it!"

"Be careful, Amy," Soraya called. "It's a big one."

"Not for Sundance," Amy replied, turning her buckskin pony towards the tree-trunk.

Seeing the jump, Sundance threw his head up in excitement and plunged forward but Amy was ready for him. Her body moved effortlessly in the saddle. "Easy now," she murmured, her fingers caressing his warm neck.

The pony's golden ears flickered as he listened to her voice – and then he relaxed, his neck lowering and his mouth softening on the bit.

Amy squeezed with her legs. In five strides they reached the tree-trunk. It loomed up in front of them, massive and solid. Amy felt Sundance's muscles bunch as he met the take-off stride perfectly and gracefully rose into the air. Amy caught a glimpse of thick, gnarled bark flashing by beneath them, felt a moment of suspension as if she and Sundance were flying, and then heard the sweet thud of his hooves as he landed cleanly on the other side. They were over!

"Good boy!" Amy cried in delight.

"That was so cool!" Soraya said, letting Jasmine trot forward to meet them. "He's jumping better than ever, Amy."

"I know!" Amy grinned, patting Sundance's neck. "He's incredible!"

As the two ponies reached each other, Jasmine stretched out her neck to say hello. With an angry squeal, Sundance threw his head in the air, his ears back. "Stop it, Sundance!" Amy exclaimed, turning him away. "Jasmine's your friend."

The buckskin nuzzled her leg affectionately. He was bad-tempered with most horses and people, but adored Amy. She had first seen him at a horse-sale. Thin and unhappy, he attacked anyone who tried to come through the gate of his pen, until Amy had persuaded her mom to buy him. They took him back to Heartland, where Amy gradually gained his trust and affection.

"Have you got any shows planned for him?" Soraya asked, as they started along the trail again.

Amy shook her head. "There's just no time. All the stalls have been full since the open day and there's a waiting list of people who want to bring their horses to us."

Just two weeks ago, Lou had organized an open day at Heartland. People had been invited to come along and find out about the methods that Heartland used to cure physically and emotionally damaged horses. Amy, and Ty — Heartland's seventeen-year-old stable-hand — had given demonstrations, and the day had been a great success. Ever since then, they had been inundated with enquiries from owners with problem horses.

"It's good that you've got lots of horses boarding, though," Soraya said. "I mean, it must be such a relief to know that you can carry on your mom's work and not stress too much about money."

Amy nodded, mulling over the difficulties Heartland had faced before the open day. After her mom had died, Heartland had come close to shutting down because of the lack of customers and funding, but now, thankfully, it was different. Business was booming.

"Yeah, I'm glad we're busy," she said. "Even if it does mean that I don't have much time to compete." She patted Sundance's neck. "Still, I guess things may start getting easier now Ben will be working for us."

Ben was the eighteen-year-old nephew of Lisa Stillman, the wealthy and successful owner of Fairfield Arabian Stud. After Amy had cured one of Fairfield's show horses, Lisa had been so impressed that she had arranged for Ben to come and work at Heartland in order for him to learn their methods. He was due to arrive that afternoon.

Soraya glanced at Amy. "Do you reckon he's got a girlfriend?"

"Why?" Amy grinned. "Are you interested?" She and Soraya had both met Ben when he had dropped off the problem horse that Amy had treated. Tall and good-looking, he had seemed OK — although not really Amy's type.

"You have to admit he *is* cute," Soraya said. She raised her eyebrows. "Poor guy. I guess he's not going to know anyone round here. Maybe I'll just *have* to offer to show him around."

Amy feigned innocence. "Don't put yourself out, Soraya. I'm sure Ty can do it — he's looking forward to having another guy around the place."

"Oh *no*," Soraya said quickly. "I'm sure I'd make a *much* better guide than Ty."

"Well, I'm looking forward to seeing Ben's horse," Amy

said. "He's a show-jumper. Ben said he'd only work at Heartland if he could come too."

"So what time's he arriving?" Soraya asked.

"Two o'clock."

Soraya glanced at her watch. "We should get a move on then. It's almost one-thirty."

Amy gathered up her reins. "What are you waiting for? Let's go!"

Amy and Soraya rode down the trail that led to the back of Heartland. Coming out of the trees, they could see Heartland's barns and sheds spread out before them – the turn-out paddocks with their dark wooden fencing, the two training rings, the twelve-stall back barn, and the front stable block that made an L-shape with the white, weather-boarded farmhouse.

As Amy halted Sundance she heard the sound of hooves thudding angrily against the wall of the barn.

"Steady now!" Ty's raised voice could be heard from inside the barn. "Easy, girl!"

"It sounds like Ty could use some help," she said.

"You go," Soraya said. "I'll see to Sundance."

"Thanks." Amy threw Sundance's reins at her friend and headed into the barn. A wide aisle separated the six stalls on each side. From a stall near the back came the crash of hooves striking the wall. Amy realised it was Dancer's stall.

Dancer was a paint mare who had been half starved and

left on a tiny patch of land. When the animal charity that had found her called them, Amy and Ty had immediately agreed to help. The mare had arrived two days ago and her treatment was progressing slowly.

"You OK, Ty?" Amy called.

Ty looked over Dancer's half-door. His dark hair was dishevelled. "Just about," he replied, wiping his bare forearm across his face.

"What's up?" Amy asked, looking into the stall. Dancer was standing by the back wall, her body trembling.

"All I did was pick up her hoof and she just went crazy," Ty said, shaking his head. "She broke her lead-rope and started acting like she was trying to kick the stall down. She had me cornered for a few moments, but luckily she didn't get me. Now she's in a total state."

Amy looked at the frightened mare. "How about using some chestnut powder to calm her down," she suggested, remembering it had been one of her mom's favourite remedies for upset horses.

Ty nodded. "Good idea. You wait with her while I fetch it," he said, and then hurried off.

The mare shifted uneasily at the back of the stall. Her muscles were tense and her ribs stuck painfully through staring her coat. Around her face were scars where a halter had been digging into the skin, and around her fetlocks were rope burns from the too-tight hobbles that had been tied around her legs to stop her from wandering away.

"It's OK, girl," Amy said softly. "You're safe now that you're here. No one's going to hurt you any more."

The mare's ears flickered uncertainly.

Ty returned with a small tin. He handed it to Amy. "Here," he said. "It might be best if you try. Perhaps I remind her of her last owner."

Amy unscrewed the lid of the tin. Inside, there was a gritty grey powder. Taking a little, she rubbed it on to the palms of her hands. Then she stepped forward, her shoulders turned sideways to the mare, her eyes lowered.

Dancer moved nervously. Amy stopped, offered her palm for the mare to sniff, and waited.

After a few moments, the mare turned and snorted. Stretching her muzzle out towards Amy's upturned hand she breathed in, her nostrils dilating. Amy waited a few moments, and then, talking softly, she gently reached out and touched Dancer's neck with her other hand. As her fingers stroked and caressed, she felt the mare gradually begin to relax. Amy's fingers worked the mare's neck until she came to her head. When Dancer did not object, she took hold of the lead-rope.

"Good work," Ty said in a low voice. Rubbing a little of the powder on to his own palms, he approached the mare. She looked at him cautiously but then stretched out her head and let him stroke her too. "Poor girl," he said, rubbing her neck. "Your life hasn't been too great up to now, has it?"

"Well, it's going to be a lot better from here on in," Amy said.

For a moment they stood in silence, both stroking the mare.

Amy looked at the deep scars on Dancer's brown and white legs. "Maybe when you touched her feet she thought that you were going to hobble her," she suggested.

Ty nodded. "I guess we'll just have to take things slowly with her."

"As always," Amy said, smiling at him.

She didn't know what she'd do without Ty. He was so good with the horses, and after her mom had died he had taken over the running of the yard while the family came to terms with their loss. She knew they were lucky to have him. He never seemed to treat working at Heartland as just a regular job — for Ty it was a way of life.

Ty looked at the tin in his hand. "Your mom's magic powder comes up trumps again."

Amy nodded. Her mom had been told about the powder by an old horseman in Tennessee. It contained herbs ground up with chestnut trimmings — the horny growths that grew on the inside of horse's legs, and were snipped off by the farrier when they grew too long. Marion, her mom, had noted down the recipe and they had used it at Heartland ever since.

"Your mom was amazing," Ty said, turning the tin over in his hands. "She knew so much. Sometimes I wonder if I'll ever be as good as her, if I'll ever have half as much knowledge as she did."

"You're pretty good already, Ty," Amy said in surprise.

"But not good enough," Ty said. He shook his head. "I was learning so much from her, Amy. Sometimes I feel that what I know is just the tip of an enormous iceberg. And I hate it. I can't stop thinking that if only I knew more I might be capable of helping horses more effectively."

"But you mustn't think like that, Ty," Amy said quickly. She stepped closer, wanting to let him know that she understood. "I felt the same when Pegasus was really ill and I couldn't help him. But then I realized I just had to accept that there are things I don't know and that all I can do is try my best." She paused, her eyes searching his. "You know Mom would have said the same."

Ty nodded slowly. "Yeah, I guess."

They stood for a moment, neither of them speaking.

The silence was interrupted by the sound of footsteps running down the aisle. "Hey, you guys! There's a trailer coming up the drive!" Soraya reached Dancer's door and looked over. "It's really fancy and smart. Come and check it out."

"It must be Ben," Amy said, looking at Ty.

He nodded. Leaving Dancer, they hurried down the yard. A gleaming white trailer, with green and purple stripes and a purple crest and the words "Fairfield Arabian Stud" emblazoned on the jockey door, was pulling up in front of the house. The truck stopped and Ben Stillman jumped out.

"Hi there," he said, straightening his tall frame.

Amy stepped forward. "Hi, I'm Amy Fleming. We met

when you brought Promise over here for your aunt. This is my friend, Soraya Martin," she said, pushing Soraya forward.

"Hi," Soraya grinned.

"Yeah, I remember." Ben smiled. "Hi."

"And you've met Ty," Amy said.

"Welcome to Heartland." Ty offered his hand.

As they shook hands, the farmhouse door opened and Lou came out. She too had met Ben when he'd dropped Promise off at Heartland. "Hello again," she said, smiling at Ben.

"Good to meet you properly this time," Ben said.

"I'll see you later – I'm just off into town," Lou said, walking off towards her car.

Just then, from inside the trailer came the sound of a horse stamping impatiently.

"Sounds like Red wants to get out," Ben said.

"Here, I'll give you a hand," Ty volunteered.

Ben disappeared inside the trailer while Ty unbolted the ramp. Amy watched eagerly, wondering what Ben's horse would be like.

Ty lowered the ramp to the ground. There was a clatter of hooves and suddenly a bright chestnut horse shot nervously down the ramp, with Ben holding tightly on to the end of its lead-rope. Once out, the horse stopped dead and looked around, his head held high.

"Wow!" Amy exclaimed. "He's gorgeous!"

"He's called Red," Ben said, looking pleased. "He's a Thoroughbred-Hanoverian cross."

Amy walked closer, admiring Red's handsome head, close-coupled back and strong, clean legs. Standing, she guessed, at around sixteen two hands, he looked every inch a show-jumper. "How old is he?" she asked, letting Red sniff her hand and then patting his muscular neck.

"Six," Ben said. "My aunt brought him for me when he was three." He glanced at the trailer. "I guess there are *some* advantages to having a rich aunt who's into horses."

Hearing a strange note in his voice, Amy glanced at him. For a moment she saw a look of bitterness cross his face.

"*Some* advantages?" Ty said. He was putting the ramp up and obviously hadn't seen Ben's expression. "That's the understatement of the year!"

"Yeah." Ben coughed, his face suddenly clearing and his voice becoming light again. "I guess you're right. So, which stall should I put him in?" he asked Amy.

"The one at the end," Amy replied, pointing towards the stable block. "It's all bedded down ready for him."

Ben clicked his tongue and Red moved forward.

Leaving Soraya and Ty to sort out the trailer, Amy went on ahead of Ben and opened the stall door. "Do you compete much on Red?" she asked.

Ben nodded as he set about taking off the wraps that had protected the gelding's legs on the journey over. "He's got real talent. I've been taking him in Prelim Jumper classes, but with the way he's been winning I figure he's going to upgrade real quick." He stood up with the wraps in his arms.

"We're going to make it to the top," he said confidently. "I'm sure of it."

Amy looked at him in surprise; he didn't sound like he had any doubts.

"So," Ben said, walking out of the stall. "What's it like living in this area?"

"OK," Amy replied.

"You'll have to show me around," Ben said.

Amy remembered what Soraya had said and saw the perfect opportunity. "Well, I'm always pretty busy with the horses," she said, as they walked down the yard towards where Soraya and Ty were standing by the trailer. "But Soraya has loads of spare time."

"Did I hear my name?" Soraya said, turning to face them.

"Yeah, I was just telling Ben that you'd be happy to show him around," Amy answered, giving her a meaningful look.

"Yeah, of course!" Soraya said, stepping forward eagerly. "Any time."

"Thanks." Ben smiled at her. "I might just take you up on that."

"Do you want to see round the yard?" Amy offered. "You've got all the horses to meet and then we can start telling you about our work here at Heartland."

"Actually, you know, I might leave all that sort of stuff till tomorrow," Ben said, yawning. "I could do with going back to my lodgings and unpacking. Then I think I'll just crash for a while."

"Oh … right," Amy said, a bit taken aback. She knew that if she was about to start work at a new yard then the first thing she would want to do was to look at the horses. "Well, sure. Go ahead."

"Great," Ben said. "Well, I'll just unload Red's kit, then I'll be off."

Amy, Ty and Soraya helped him carry the mountain of rugs, tack and grooming kit up to the tack-room and then Ben unhitched the trailer and got into the truck. "I'll be back to feed Red later," he said, starting the engine.

Not long after he had driven off, Lou got back. "I think I just passed Ben on the road. Has he gone already?" she asked, getting out of her car.

Amy nodded.

"But I was going to ask him if he wanted to stay for supper tonight," Lou said, frowning. "Oh well, I guess I can give him a call. I've got his phone number." She looked at Soraya and Ty. "You're both welcome to stay too."

"That would be great," Ty said. "Thanks."

"Unfortunately, I can't," Soraya said ruefully. "I'm going out tonight for my mom's birthday. But thanks anyway, Lou."

Lou looked down the drive. "It's a bit odd that Ben didn't stick around for longer. I thought he'd be here for hours. Grandpa will be sorry to have missed him." Shaking her head, she went back into the house.

"So what do you think of him?" Amy asked Ty and Soraya,

as they walked back up the yard.

"Definitely cute!" Soraya enthused.

"And after all, what else matters?" Ty teased.

Soraya pretended to punch him.

Amy grinned. "Come on, what do you think, Ty?"

"He seems fine," Ty said, shrugging.

"Yes ... and?" Amy pushed for more

"And nothing," Ty said. He looked at Amy's and Soraya's expectant faces. "Well, what else do you expect me to say?" he demanded. "I've only met the guy for about five minutes."

"Well, I've only met him for five minutes too and I think he seems really nice," Amy said. She turned to Soraya. "He was telling me about Red. He's been competing in Prelim Jumpers. Ben thinks they'll upgrade pretty quick."

"I wonder when we'll get to see him ride," Soraya said. Her eyes looked dreamy. "He's so fit and athletic!"

Ty grimaced. "Oh, please!" Rolling his eyes at them, he went into the tack-room.

Exchanging grins, Amy and Soraya followed him. In the middle of the tack-room floor was a mound of Ben's stuff.

"Three saddles," Ty commented, starting to make space on the already crowded saddle racks.

"And all top quality," Amy added, picking up a forward-cut jumping saddle and admiring the supple, well-oiled leather.

"I wish I had a rich aunt who would buy me a horse like Red and all this stuff," Soraya said.

Ty nodded as he hung up a bridle. "Ben sure is a lucky guy."

Amy thought about the look she had seen pass across Ben's face just after he'd unloaded Red. At that moment he hadn't seemed exactly thrilled with his good fortune. Still, it must have been wonderful to have grown up on a huge stud farm with lots of money. Perhaps he'd just found it difficult leaving Fairfield and was feeling upset with his aunt. "Imagine living at a place like Fairfield," she said out loud.

"Yeah," Ty said nodding. "I wish."

Amy looked at him. Ty's family had very little money. To help out his parents he had first started working as a part-time stable-hand at Heartland when he was just fifteen. Then he had left school a year later, when he was offered a full-time position by Marion Fleming.

"Do you know why Ben grew up with his aunt instead of his parents?" Soraya asked.

"I think it was something to do with his parents getting divorced when he was younger," Amy said, remembering a conversation between Lou and Lisa Stillman when they'd first discussed the possibility of Ben coming to Heartland. "But I don't really know that much about it. Still, I guess we might find out more tonight."

"I wish I could stay," Soraya said longingly. "Promise you'll find out all the gossip about him – like whether he's got a girlfriend or not."

"Oh, you mean the really *important* stuff?" Amy grinned at her. "Don't worry, of course I will!"